FIELDS OF ARAGON

Kelvin Hughes

Copyright © 2020 Kelvin Hughes

The right of Kelvin Hughes to be identified as the author of this book has been asserted by him in accordance with the Copyright, Designs and Patents Act 1988.

All Rights Reserved.

This is a work of fiction.

All characters, names and places in this story are the product of the writer's imagination or are used fictitiously. Any resemblance to actual persons, living or dead, is purely coincidental.

For
Sylvia Dobón
(before, now, always…)

FOREWORD

After the loss of Teruel during the freezing winter of 1937-38, the British Battalion was at its base in Tarrazona de la Mancha. Here they hoped for some much-needed rest and a chance to recover from the hardships they had endured. Little did they know that things were about to get worse, a lot worse.

At the beginning of March 1938, Franco launched a massive offensive on the Aragon Front, with the aim of driving a wedge into the remaining Republican zone and cutting it into two by reaching the Mediterranean. If he could achieve this, he would separate Catalunya from the Republican government in Valencia.

It had been assumed that the Nationalist forces would be just as exhausted as their Republican counterparts after the Battle of Teruel, and therefore a further attack on the Aragon Front was considered unlikely.

However, Franco had quickly amassed a new army and attacked using blitzkrieg tactics, along a front running from the Pyrenees down to Teruel. Several early breakthroughs were made in the Republican defences and the Rebels advanced deep into Government territory in a matter of days. The Republican army was soon in full retreat…

CHAPTER ONE

The creaking lorry carried us through the night. At some stage, despite the extreme cold, I must have fallen asleep. I know that, because I awoke with a start, with Jack tugging at my arm.

"We're t'get out an' stretch our legs a bit Billy," he said.

For a moment I couldn't quite figure out where I was, and then, of course, I remembered that we were in Spain. In the back of a battered old lorry, under a tarpaulin cover. We were on the way from Barcelona to a place I'd never heard of, called Albacete. All the foreigners got sent there apparently. There were seven of us in the lorry. Two Brits and the rest were French, I think. Nobody had spoken much during the journey. The air in the lorry smelt of stale cigarettes and human sweat despite the cold.

I jumped down from the tailgate and took a deep breath of fresh air. It was almost dawn. The air was frigid, a chilly mist hung all around. I could make out some stunted pine trees close by and see the red rocks beside the road. Jack was already lighting a cigarette. He took a few drags and then offered it to me even though he knew I didn't smoke. I guess he thought that one day soon I would want to start.

It was Jack who had got me into this. He was a year older than me, and I looked up to him as if he were my big brother. He had taken me under his wing when I had started work on the building site in South London. I was straight out of school, just turned fourteen. Jack had already been working there a year and knew the ropes. Without him, I think the older men would have eaten me alive. He taught me how to always look busy, how to always be polite to the foreman and how to make a half hour job last a whole day.

When my grandmother died, just after my sixteenth birthday, it was natural enough that Jack and I would find digs together. My grandmother had been the only family I had ever known. My father had died of gas poisoning in the Great War and my mother had joined him three months later whilst giving birth to me. I sometimes hated myself for her death.

My grandmother had brought me up as best she could, always one step away from destitution. Just before her death, she had given me a photograph of my parents on their wedding day, it was the only way I had ever known them. It was the only worthwhile possession I had.

Jack and I shared a little back room in an old terraced house, owned by a widow, who desperately needed our rent money to survive. She prepared us frugal meals that barely kept us alive and some nights she would take Jack to her bedroom to keep her company. I always knew when that was going to happen because she would give him a slightly larger portion of food. At my expense. I wouldn't have minded keeping her company for a while if it meant an extra ladle of soup or half a dumpling more, but she only ever asked Jack.

It was understandable. Jack was tall and lean. He had thick dark hair and he was a year older than me. When we told her we had joined the Communist Party and were leaving for the war in Spain, she had burst into tears. Maybe it was because she would no longer have our weekly rent money, but I like to think it was because she genuinely liked us, or at least she liked Jack.

She made us a sandwich each for the journey and watched us leave as we walked off towards the underground.

All I'd heard of Spain, was what the men at work said as they drank their tea. There had been a Fascist uprising and a civil war had broken out. Then, one by one, the men started to disappear from the site. The reason behind their sudden departure was always the same – he's gone to fight in Spain.

One day Jack told me that he had decided to join the Communist Party and head for the war in Spain. He said I ought to join too. I didn't hesitate. We went to their offices and I let him do the explaining. He'd obviously heard other men talking about what to do and say. We passed the interview and a few weeks later we were en route to Paris.

We'd spent our last savings on a new pair of boots each, it was the best decision we ever made. And dressed in our Sunday best and acting all self-assured and cocky, we left to go to war. It wasn't half as easy as I had assumed it would be. In Paris they gave us a half-hearted medical and another interview and gave us the option to change our minds if we wanted to. We didn't want to, or at least Jack didn't want us to.

We crossed the Pyrenees on a desperately cold night in early February. My feet were frozen solid despite my new boots and both my pairs of socks. It was the longest night of my life. Added to the cold was the fear, since we were illegally crossing the border into a country at war. All the while as a silent snow fell, I just stared at Jack's back as we climbed ever higher, following our French guide who never spoke a word except to swear if he stumbled on the rocky goat track.

Come the morning, we were in Spain and the next day in Barcelona. It seemed a quite well-organised route, and I wondered just how many other young men had gone this way before us. I wondered how many were dead now. Maybe we would soon be dead. Jack had promised to look after me, just as he always had done on the building site, and I took great comfort in that. He had never let me down.

From Albacete we were sent to Tarazona de la Mancha for training. It was a bleak and frozen village lost somewhere on the way to Cuenca. It seemed almost as if it had died, and few civilians remained. We were put into a long, low stone building with other members of the XVth Brigade who had survived the recent defeat at Teruel. At night, as the wind howled around outside, looking for someone to murder, they talked in hushed voices of what they had been through. They complained that with better equipment and better artillery support, things might have been different. They mentioned as little as possible those who had been left behind.

We were woken early, by someone who seemed to be in charge and tumbled out into the slushy street to begin our training. We ambled to the main square dominated by the old church, and then spent a long while learning how to march as a unit. The old hands laughed and joked and deliberately messed things up, so that we had to start all over again. The next morning, only the newest arrivals were taken to the square to practice marching. We were issued with wooden rifles and drilled until our feet hurt from blisters rather than from the cold which was at least a change. We threw stones to practice using grenades.

Food arrived on a lorry every evening just before dark. Almost certainly, it had come from Albacete, which explained why the food was cold when we finally got our small portion slopped into our mess tins. Everything was cold in Tarazona de la Mancha. The food was often just tough old beans in some sort of oily gravy, but I had quickly learned to stomach it. There was no alternative and, as an eighteen-year-old, I could have eaten a whole horse and still have wanted more. Horse would have been a luxury for sure. Donkey would have been good. Sometimes we were given lentils or chickpea soup as a special treat. I wondered what the few remaining civilians left in Tarazona de la Mancha got to eat. It probably didn't bear thinking about.

At night, we lay shivering in our stone barracks. The old hands had the places nearest to the fire, taking it in turns to feed its voracious appetite for wood. I found myself watching the flakes of snow, that forced themselves through the gaps in the roof tiles, to die for a moment of comparative warmth that was, just for a brief instant, being on the inside. I longed for the morning to come and the endless marching to start so that I might feel alive again. Every night in that place was a long death.

Some comrades began to return to the Brigade after a stay in hospital. These were the heroes of Jarama or

Brunete or Guadalajara or Teruel. Those who had escaped death by the skin of their teeth and had now been declared well enough to have the chance to die for the Republic once more. They looked fit and well-fed compared to the rest. Their clothes were cleaner. In the afternoons, as we lay exhausted on our beds, they talked about tactics and told us of the horrors of bombardment or worse still of bombing attacks by aeroplanes.

At the beginning of March, the weather improved enough for us to be taken out of the town and shown how to dig ourselves into the hard ground. We also learnt how to form rudimentary trenches. We were taught to advance on an enemy position under fire although there was no firing of course. Our weapons still hadn't arrived. I remember thinking it would be a great day when I finally got to fire a gun for the first time. It was all I aspired to.

*

That night, with the lorry delivering our food, came news of the war. It was unexpected news. The Rebels had launched an attack all along the Aragon Front. The situation was desperate. You didn't have to be an experienced soldier to know that it meant we would soon be called into battle.

The mood in the barracks changed immediately. Gone were the complaints about everything, gone were the jokes and camaraderie. Men lay on their mattresses smoking or gazing at photographs of their loved ones. Many were scribbling a last letter like crazy. I had no one to write to. Those who were lucky enough to have weapons from earlier battles lovingly dismantled them and cleaned them and put them back together and then started all over again.

I just lay there listening to Jack. He hadn't stopped talking since we had come inside to clean our mess tins. Everyone ate standing together around the food lorry, just in case there might be the chance of a second helping. There never was.

Jack talked about the possibility of seeing his first Fascist up close. Of the possibility of killing his first Fascist. I wasn't sure I could kill anyone, I wasn't sure at all, but I kept that to myself. If it came down to a choice of kill or be killed, then I hoped that instinct would take over. I would need to learn to shoot a rifle first though.

That last night, in the freezing barracks at Tarazona de la Mancha, I hardly slept at all. What if the Rebels had broken through and could reach us there during the night? I was glad I had chosen to sleep in my uniform, although almost everyone did. It was an attempt to keep out the cold. The only good thing about the freezing weather, according to our more experienced comrades, was that the lice problem was less than in warmer times. Even so, I itched like hell and had scratched most of my body red raw.

If the Fascists arrived before dawn, then we had few weapons to fight them. At least I would die with my clothes on, that was the only consolation I could think of at that moment. What if we were captured prisoner? We had heard the stories of what the Nationalists did to foreigners. It was better to die than be captured alive I had decided.

At dawn, some lorries arrived. We heard their squealing brakes, and everyone was suddenly up and moving about. Those who had weapons were feeling for them. Those of us who did not, were pulling on boots and scarves ready to face the cold more than the enemy.

CHAPTER TWO

The lorries were ours. They brought weapons and other basic supplies. Now, no one could be in any doubt that we were going to be thrown into the fray, and soon. The lorries stayed, their drivers standing around smoking. Everyone was waiting for an order to come to direct us to one place or another. In the meantime, those of us without a weapon were allocated one, and told to keep it close as if it were our girlfriend. I'd never had a girlfriend, but one day when I did, I vowed to keep her close, as if she were my rifle.

The rifle fascinated me. It was strange to finally get to hold one in my hands. We were given a few rounds of ammunition and a basic firing range was set up in a field not far from the barracks. The first time I pulled the trigger, I almost dropped the thing in fright. Jack laughed at me. Then he tried himself, and it wasn't so funny anymore. How were we supposed to control this deadly beast, let alone make it do our will? Imagine trying to fire it in the heat of battle.

All around us, men were doing better than we were. Some had a bit of military experience most had fired a gun before. The old hands made it look easy.

In the end, Jack and I were considered more of a danger to our own side than the enemy, and we were assigned to a machinegun squad. There were three of us. An older man called Walt, who was also from London, was put in charge. He was big and strong and would carry and fire the heavy gun. Jack was to carry the tripod on which the gun rested, and I was given the job of carrying the ammunition.

When he first saw us, Walt screwed his face up in disgust.

"So, now I'm a fuckin' babysitter, am I?" he moaned.

Personally, I was rather pleased to think that I wouldn't be required to kill anyone. It was clear that Walt was the one who would be doing all the killing.

The three of us went out into the fields and Walt set about learning how to use the gun. Jack and I pretended to be interested. At last he got the damn thing to fire and seemed satisfied. We trudged back to the barracks.

*

It was late afternoon when some more lorries arrived along with our orders. We were to be rushed to a place called Belchite, which was on the point of being overrun. In the jolting lorry, someone explained that the town of Belchite had been captured at the end of the previous summer at the cost of many lives. Now it was in danger of once more falling into Fascist hands.

I remember sitting there in the lorry, as it jolted along a difficult road, feeling a gentle shaking overcoming my muscles. At first, I just put it down to the vibrations of the lorry, but slowly as it got worse, I had to admit that it was my body reacting to the fact that we were about to go into battle. I held my hands tightly together and clamped my knees shut and closed my eyes, desperately trying to think of other places and other things. I felt an attack of nausea slowing spreading out from my stomach.

The excited chatter at the start of the journey slowly disappeared. Silence reigned as the miles ticked painfully away. I did not know how far we had to go, I just hoped it would be far enough for my body to regain control of itself. I wondered if Jack was going through the same thing. Probably not, I decided, he never seemed to get nervous about anything at all.

The lorry slowed down and eventually stopped and my heart leapt into my mouth. It was just a break for us to stretch our legs. All around, the members of the XVth Brigade were milling slowly about. Some disappeared into the scrub to relieve themselves. Most were lighting up cigarettes. We all had our rifles slung loosely over our shoulders, just in case. How far could we be from the front? I noticed that it was nearly dark, I really didn't want my first taste of combat to be at night. I couldn't hear the sound of artillery though, so I guessed we weren't near yet.

After half an hour or so, we climbed back into the lorries and set off once more.

"How far to go?" I asked Walt.

"How should I kno'?"

"Don't worry Billy mate," whispered Jack and he squeezed my arm. "We'll be al'right."

The lorry drove on, into the night. We dozed since there was nothing else to do. In the moments when I found myself awake, I strained my ears to see if I could hear the sound of guns. The good thing was that my body had calmed down and I was no longer shaking. I was worried that it might start up again when we reached our destination, but there was nothing I could do about that, I would just have to wait and see.

During the night, the temperature dropped, and my teeth started chattering. I kept my mouth closed so no one would hear, and when we made a second longer stop, I tried jumping on the spot in order to warm up a bit. It didn't do much good. In the end, I just gave up and went to stand next to Jack and saw him shivering, just as miserable as I was. We didn't talk, just stood there, hands in pockets, our breath smoking.

*

Just before dawn, we finally arrived. We didn't enter Belchite but were dropped outside. We stood around in the half-light until someone arrived to tell us to take up positions on some high ground just beyond the town. An attack was expected at dawn and we had arrived late. We filed quickly through Belchite, which was mostly in ruins from the previous battle, and moved towards the high ground we had been directed to defend. There were soldiers milling all around, going to and from the town. Some carrying ammunition, others hurrying with orders. There was a definite sense of urgency, as if something important was about to happen.

Once we reached the high ground, jutting out of the midst of a pine forest, we found some Americans there which was comforting. We took up positions in the centre, the Americans moved to our left and to the right were a small, ragged-looking, group of Spaniards. One of them explained very patiently, to one of our comrades who spoke a little Spanish, that they had been fleeing from the enemy for the last twenty-four hours and were exhausted.

There was little cover, and we dug in as best we could, scraping small indentations in which to lie when the enemy came. We didn't have to wait long. As soon as there was enough light to see properly, an artillery barrage began. I jumped half out of my skin when the first shell exploded somewhere in front of us. It caught me totally unprepared. The noise was amazing, and it set all my nerves jangling. It was as if your very brain had exploded inside your head.

Then the next shell arrived, and the next. Each one creeping a little closer to where we were. At any moment I expected the men around me to jump to their feet and run away. To run back to the lorries and get the hell out of this madness. Suddenly, Tarrazona de la Mancha seemed like some small heaven.

A shell exploded right in front of us, spraying us with small stones and whipping up a dust storm. We covered our heads with our hands as best we could. The Spanish troops had hard helmets, but we didn't, nor did the Americans. Not that a helmet would save you from a direct hit mind you. Then the American position took a strike, and for the first time I saw men blown to pieces in front of my eyes. One second they were there lying folded into the hard ground, and the next there was just a tangled red mass of flesh.

"Planes!" came a shout. We all looked skywards at the approaching black objects that were quickly approaching. I had never seen a plane before and was quite intrigued, until I noticed that one of the men a little to my right had started praying. He was mumbling the Lord's Prayer, maybe it was the only one he knew.

The planes came ever closer, dropping ever lower. It was clear that they were heading for our position here on the exposed high ground. Suddenly, they were diving down towards us. I heard them screaming and noticed black crosses painted on their wings, and I buried my head under my arms as the others were doing all around me and pressed myself as deep into the ground as I could. The bombs started falling. They seemed almost to drop on top of us, but I suppose they couldn't have been. How long it went on for I cannot say. It seemed forever. At last, the explosions ended, and the planes droned quickly away, back from where they had come. The artillery barrage meanwhile had continued, although it had faded into the background whilst we suffered the attack by the planes. I raised my head just slightly to look around me. The Spanish troops had been blown to hell. A few lay moaning and screaming, but most had been reduced to shattered bodies and missing limbs. I felt sick to my stomach. I remember my body trembling and my ears ringing. Yet even so, I heard a new sound make an appearance. It was like the chattering of a million teeth all at once. I was still wondering what it might be, when the air above my head seemed to be swarming with buzzing insects.

"Machineguns," hissed Walt. "Keep yer 'eads down."

The machinegun squads had obviously got into position under cover of the barrage and were close enough to keep us pinned down. This wasn't a fight, I decided, it was a massacre. At that moment, I cursed myself for leaving London. Why had I listened to Jack? What an idiot I was. I was going to die there on that hill, as men all around me were doing, within weeks of entering Spain, without the slightest contribution to the cause. It all seemed such a futile waste.

I would have died too, if someone hadn't had the sense to pull us out of there before the infantry arrived to finish us off. I for one didn't need to be told twice. As soon as someone shouted "retreat," I was up and running. I ran as fast as I could, my boots throwing up stones and gravel. It seemed like I was slipping and falling all the time. I did fall a couple of times such was my haste. But I wasn't the fastest. Men ran past me and I found myself panicking about being left behind on my own.

I glanced back and was relieved to see Walt just behind me, struggling to run whilst carrying the heavy machinegun. I wondered why he hadn't just left it. I couldn't see Jack. It occurred to me that he might have been hit and was lying back up the hill wounded, crying out for his friend who had abandoned him. But I didn't turn back. Nothing on earth could have made me return to that hell. The top of the hill must have been blown right off as rocks and stones flew all around us, some flying clean over our heads.

I ran until I thought my lungs would burst right out of my body. I reached the bottom of the hill where someone was trying to put some order into our retreat. We fanned out, rifles levelled pointing back toward the high ground. We began a more orderly retreat, walking backwards as quickly as we could.

There was a low stone wall next to the road back to Belchite, and we were told to set up our machinegun to give covering fire to allow other survivors to reach the safety of the town. I was still trembling violently, and my face was thick with dust. My throat was dry, and my eyes burned. My ears were ringing. But I was glad to have something to do. Jack had joined us. I don't know where he had been and there wasn't time to ask.

We set up the machinegun on top of the wall and waited. I was sweating and shaking, but Walt seemed calmness personified, his eyes trying to see through the dust and smoke for a first glimpse of the enemy. Jack and I looked too but saw nothing.

We waited about ten minutes until Walt decided that surely the others had reached the safety of the town, and then he snatched up the big gun and we were half walking, half running back along the road into Belchite.

We entered via the Plaza del Pozo and went to find our company. It took us a while. Everything was confused given the haste of our retreat. Those of us who had returned from the high ground eventually mixed in with those who had set up defensive positions on that side of town near the road to Zaragoza. Walt led us into a house, and we climbed the stairs to find a good vantage point to set up our gun once again. The roof had been blown in, and in the attic space we were able to set up. I remember thinking that we would be a sitting duck for the planes when they came, but Walt didn't seem to have thought of that, and I just kept quiet.

"You al'right?" Jack whispered. I couldn't reply my throat was too dry to speak. I tried to give him a smile, but it must just have been some sort of weird grimace. He squeezed my arm.

Soon the first Fascist troops appeared in the distance. They were advancing slowly towards our position coming out of the smoke and confusion.

"Hold your fire!" came an order. "Let 'em get nice an' close."

We waited. The Fascists got ever closer. They must have thought that we had abandoned the town and carried on running, but suddenly the order came to fire and we opened up with all that we had. At last, we were fighting back. I watched, amazed, as the crouching figures that had been coming along the road towards us suddenly seemed to fold at the knees and drop to the ground. A few managed to turn and run, but most were cut down. We stopped firing. We had been told not to waste ammunition as it was a scarce commodity on our side.

Then the planes returned.

CHAPTER THREE

Walt realised the danger we were in as soon as he heard the planes. Cursing everyone he could think of, he picked up the heavy machinegun and started back towards the stairs leading down from the roof. He didn't need to tell us to follow him, we were right behind. I stumbled a few times on the stairs which were badly broken in places, but we were soon out of the building and into the sunshine.

"Where the bloody hell do you chaps think you're going?" came an angry voice of authority from behind us.

The next second, we heard the screaming dive of the attacking planes and the only thing that mattered was to put as much distance as possible between ourselves and the tumble-down house where we had been moments before.

There was a loud whoosh, and the air seemed to be sucked out of our lungs. Dust and dirt rained down on us, but we kept running. Several other huge explosions followed.

When we had finally run far enough to feel safe, we turned to look back. The house where we had been just moments before was gone, just a pile of useless rubble remained. The houses on either side had met a similar fate except that the one to the right had one wall remaining. You could see the twisted round wooden beams jutting out of the walls, and strangely enough, some light blue tiles still stuck to the kitchen wall. The stone sink was gone. The voice of authority was gone too. Everyone who had been there was gone.

As we watched, a figure emerged from the dust. He was staggering and his body was mostly naked since his uniform had been blown nearly clean off. He saw us and tried to walk in our direction, but then he toppled forward, twitched once and lay dead.

"Shit!" said Walt. "We're really in trouble now."

We hurried past the abandoned and roofless church and down a sloping street towards the main square. Most of the houses had been reduced to rubble, but on the corner of the square one remained nearly intact. It was here that the retreating troops seemed to be heading in order to form a new line of resistance. When we reached the building, which was a large four-story family house, we were ordered to set up behind a low sandbag barricade. Our job was to protect this new temporary headquarters for as long as possible. The building had been the headquarters of the Falange before the first battle of Belchite, and their symbol of the yoke and five arrows was still visible painted in black on the front wall. Next to this building was the Ayuntamiento, but it was on fire having already received a direct hit.

On the side wall of the big house, was a large painted sign that proclaimed the name of the square as Plaza de la República. I didn't think it was going to belong to the Republic much longer. The real name plaque said it was Plaza Nueva.

Runners were sent for ammunition and to beg for grenades. Walt told me to go with them and bring back some belts for our machinegun. I hurried after the other three who had been sent, desperate not to get lost. As it turned out, there just seemed to be one endless long street that led towards the Arco de la Villa. Beyond the archway was the square, where the lorries had dropped us when we had arrived that morning. It seemed so long ago now.

The street, the Calle Mayor, climbed upwards and we hurried as fast as we could. Once out of the town through the stone archway, we found the square almost deserted. A couple of lorries remained with ammunition, but their engines were running, and their drivers were itching to get away.

There were no grenades. There were never any grenades complained one of the others with a heavy Welsh accent. The other three carried a box of ammunition each, and I found some machinegun belts and draped them around my neck and shoulders and staggered back under their weight.

As we walked back down the slope of the Calle Mayor, we heard excited gunfire. The battle had resumed once more. We started to run, as best we could. At last, we reached the square. The Rebels had taken over the derelict houses on the far side, and some had even rushed to take up positions behind the stone fountain, although these were pinned down for the moment.

"Thank fuck!" exclaimed Walt. "We're almost out of ammo."

Jack grabbed one of the belts from around my neck, almost strangling me in his haste to get it ready to be fed into the greedy gun. As soon as Walt had fired off the remaining bullets from the previous belt, he tried to insert the new belt into the empty gun. It wouldn't fit.

"Give me that you fuckin' idiot," shouted Walt in his face. But Walt couldn't make it fit either.

"Why don't it fit?" asked Jack.

"You stupid shit!" shouted Walt at me. "You've gone an' brought the wrong sort."

"What?" I asked.

"This ain't the right bloody ammo belt. You useless piece of shit! Go get the right sort. Take this." He threw the last belt he had been able to fire from the gun at me. I hurried off back up the street towards the Arco de la Villa in the distance, as fast as I could run.

It had never occurred to me that there might be more than one type of ammunition for a machinegun. I really was useless. Behind me, Jack and Walt were making do with their rifles, but a machinegun would have been so much better to keep the Fascists at bay. It was suddenly as if the whole course of the battle, indeed the whole course of the war hung on my ability to get back to them with the right type of ammunition. If we could hold back the nationalists until nightfall, maybe reinforcements would arrive.

When I reached the Arco de la Villa, I found the square beyond deserted. The last two lorries had gone. I could see men streaming away along the road out of Belchite. The town was being abandoned. And yet, back inside the walls, there was still some resistance taking place. It was a futile resistance though by now.

I could have fled. I could have just turned my back on Belchite and the Spanish Republic, neither of them meant anything to me after all. But I couldn't turn my back on Jack. Walt might kill me, but I had to let Jack know that not only was there no further machinegun ammunition, but that the town was fast being abandoned. The only thing we could sensibly do was to get as far away as possible before the main bulk of the Rebel army arrived. Perhaps the Fascist target was just to recapture Belchite, and they would halt their advance and we would be able to regroup and form a proper defensive line somewhere else, somewhere better.

There was a steady stream of men running up the Calle Mayor now, all abandoning their positions and only concerned with saving their own lives. I dodged in and out of them. Their faces were written with fear, some were cursing as they ran. I began to wonder if the defence of the main square was already over and that I would run straight into the arms of the Fascists. Maybe Jack was already dead.

Cautiously I peered around the corner of the big house and was relieved to see the others crouching low beneath the cover of the sandbags.

"There's no more ammo," I informed them breathlessly. "Everyone's leavin'."

"Let's get the fuck out of 'ere," decided Walt. We crawled back from the low barricade and around the corner of the house, and then we slipped away from the firing, hugging the bombed-out houses of the previous battle. We retreated as quickly as we could up the Calle mayor, past the casino, constantly glancing over our shoulders. We reached the Arco de la Villa and found a group of fellow stragglers gathered there.

A young Spanish captain saw Walt's machinegun and told us to set up on the balcony above the arch, but Walt waved the empty gun at him and shouted. "No balas," a couple of times to make sure he was understood. I had left the useless ammunition behind in the Plaza de la República, there hadn't seemed any reason to carry it with me.

We quickly scavenged the wrecked houses around the Arco and managed to form a makeshift barricade of broken tables and chairs and a plump straw mattress that someone had found. We completely blocked the archway and waited for the Rebels to approach up the Calle Mayor. We had a good field of fire, but it was unlikely that they would simply advance towards us up the street. I placed my rifle on top of a table leg. I was trembling and it would help steady my aim. I glanced at Jack who was beside me. He gave me just the hint of a smile, and then we both strained our eyes ahead of us into the billowing dust, looking for the enemy.

It seemed like we waited forever, but it couldn't have been that long. And then we saw them, hugging the walls and keeping away from the centre of the road, flitting in and out of the smoky gloom. They were coming ever closer. We could hear them shouting encouragement to each other.

Suddenly, they rushed at us. They were a lot closer than I had expected. We started firing with our rifles. I squeezed my eyes tight shut, pulled the trigger, felt the hot breath of the weapon smack back against my face as its enormous anger kicked back against my shoulder. I opened my eyes. Then I fired again. This time I kept my eyes open, but I don't think I hit anyone.

We had done enough. The charge ran out of impetus and the Fascists turned and fled back to the cover of the gloom and the walls of the houses. It was a small moment of victory in a long day of defeat, but it didn't last long. We soon became aware of noise away to our right, as some of their soldiers were making holes in the internal walls between houses. They were trying to get from one to the other, trying to outflank us. It was time to retreat again. The little Spanish captain made a gesture with his head to indicate to Walt that we should get the hell out, and we sprinted away from the archway across the deserted square. I looked back and saw the little captain, pistol in hand, firing shots into the dust cloud, trying to give the impression that there were still men defending the last barricade. And then someone threw a grenade and the captain was gone and the Rebels were storming through.

We were half-way across the square. I felt the hiss of a bullet close to my right cheek and doubled my pace. There was a low stone wall on the far side of the square, and it saved our lives. We dived over it and were quickly able to fire back at the Fascists who were pouring through the Arco de la Villa. A couple of them fell to the ground and the others, caught out in the open, turned to run back. That was our chance to escape.

We raced away from the wall, keeping low, along the road out of Belchite. We were the last to get out. No one from our side now remained fighting in that place. Jack and I took it in turns to help Walt carry the useless machinegun.

We didn't keep to the road for long, it was too dangerous. Planes might return at any moment. Instead, we veered off to the right and headed towards the hills. Every now and then we would find a frightened comrade who had run as far as he could and had dropped to the ground in exhaustion. We picked them up and encouraged them to come with us, and our group gradually increased in size. Any that were too exhausted or too badly wounded were left behind. One man was babbling like a lunatic about his mother having left him there on that Spanish hillside. We left him as well and pushed on up into the white hills through the twisted dwarf pine trees. We were desperate to put as much distance as possible between ourselves and the hell of Belchite. I remember seeing an abandoned house made of small red bricks, stones placed on what remained of its roof tiles to stop them being blown away. I wondered why we didn't hide out there, just for a few hours at least, but we pushed on.

There came a moment when sheer fatigue seemed to overcome us all at once, and as a group we collapsed to the ground panting like dogs. It was then that I realised that I hadn't had anything to drink all day. I fumbled for my water bottle and took a long gulp. It was hot and tasted of the dust from the inside of my mouth, but it helped to soothe my throat. I offered it to Jack and he drank a bit, sloshed it around his mouth, spat it out and then drank again. I offered it to Walt.

"I got somethin' better," he said with a grin. He found his own bottle and took a long swig. He offered it to Jack. After a quick sniff and a moment of doubt, Jack took a long gulp and then started coughing furiously. Walt took the bottle from him and handed it to me. Given Jack's reaction, I just took a small sip. The liquid burned my tongue, numbed my mouth and left a trail of fire down my throat. I started to cough just as Jack was doing. I heard Walt burst out laughing.

"What's that?" I gasped.

"Coñac," said Walt. "Good, ain't it?"

I went back to my water bottle and Jack produced his and drank too. Walt took another long draught of his brandy and then laughed again. He then offered it to another man sitting close by, and the foul liquid did the rounds slowly until it was all gone.

After a short rest, we got to our feet and pushed on once more. We were moving slowly now. It had been a long day and we were weary and hungry. We weren't heading in any definite direction. None of us knew the terrain. We had no map to tell us where to go. Because Jack and I accepted Walt as our leader, so the others were happy to do so as well. He walked at the front of the group, the machinegun now slung over his right shoulder, leading us to only he knew where.

Whether it was just pure luck or by some feat of miraculous judgement by Walt, we reached a larger group of fellow survivors just before nightfall. They had settled into an abandoned farm, and we huddled at the base of a stone wall to keep out of the wind and try to get some rest.

I was awoken sometime during the night to take a turn on watch, and I realised that my whole body ached. I leant on top of the wall and stared off into the darkness. There were scudding clouds blown by the wind that obscured the moon most of the time, and therefore there was little light. Sometimes I could make out the distant hills through which we had escaped, mostly I couldn't see anything at all. I willed myself to stay awake and was grateful for the cold that made my teeth chatter and kept me alert. I was just wondering how long I would have to be on sentry duty when I thought I saw something moving off in the half light.

CHAPTER FOUR

I quickly bent down and shook Walt violently. He had been sleeping at my feet and I had instructions to wake him for anything, no matter how insignificant it might seem.

"What's up?" he asked rubbing his eyes.

"There's someone out there," I whispered.

"Wake everyone up, but quietly."

I went quickly along the wall, shaking people and alerting them to the possible danger. I hoped I had been right about what I had seen, if not there were going to be a lot of pissed off people.

I returned to stand close to Walt who was peering into the gloom.

"You sure you saw somethin'?" he demanded.

"Sure," I stated, although I was anything but. What if it had been a tree bending in the wind or a wild goat or something?

Jack was on the other side of me and he saw the movement, when it came again, at the same moment as I did. We both raised our rifles to fire. Walt slapped them down.

"Don't shoot you stupid bastards," he hissed. "What if they're ours?"

I hadn't thought of that. I had just assumed that they would be Fascists.

Gradually, out of the darkness, blurred shapes began to transform into more obvious figures. They were bunched together, trudging, heads bowed. They certainly weren't fanned out rifles at the ready. Walt had made a good call. These looked like defeated men who had no idea where they were or where they were supposed to be going.

"Who goes there?" shouted Walt.

"They might be Spanish," I whispered.

"Lincoln-Washingtons," came a shout with a heavy American accent.

"Thank fuck," said Walt.

The Americans came cautiously across to our position. When they were close enough and they could see that we were really their comrades, they clambered over our low stone wall and we started to embrace each other.

"Am I sure glad to see you guys," said an American Commissar who was in charge of the group. There were nearly a hundred of them. They had been on the high ground outside of Belchite on our left at the start of the battle, they had taken a lot of casualties from the bombardment and had retreated down into the valley. They had by-passed Belchite, realising that there was no way it could be held against such over-whelming odds and retreated along the main road.

In the late afternoon, they had been attacked by planes and had scattered into the fields. Bit by bit they had regrouped and decided to get as far away from the road as possible. They had rested for a couple of hours before deciding to push on through the darkness and then try to hide up come the dawn so that they wouldn't be sitting ducks for the German Stukas that had been harassing them all day.

I was relieved of sentry duty once the Americans were settled in for what remained of the night. Jack took my place on watch. Walt said we had young keen eyes, certainly better than his.

*

We were on our feet before dawn and ready to move again. The American Commissar had decided that we should head in the general direction of the River Ebro and towards Catalunya. There was no way, he argued, that the Rebels would ever capture Catalunya. It just couldn't happen.

We climbed a hill, after an hour or so, and saw in the valley below a mass of our own troops moving slowly. They were heading in the same general direction as we had been walking. Their scouts up on the high ground had spotted us, and we were soon welcomed among them. It must have been a big relief for Walt, since there were now plenty of people who were senior to him and would make the difficult decisions.

Up on the right-hand side of the valley was another low hill, upon which were the ruins of a small castle. It had been decided that we would take up defensive positions in this valley for the best part of the day and then move on in the evening. The American Commissar came to look for us.

"You guys with the machinegun, you're to set up in that castle up on the hill. I've got to take three machineguns up there."

"No ammo mate," said Walt dismissively. The Commissar trudged off to find someone else with a machinegun and the ammunition to go with it.

The German Stukas found us around mid-morning. They circled a couple of times, checking out our position. We fired a few pathetic shots, as if that might scare them off, and then busied ourselves with trying to merge into the landscape as best we could. Walt had found us a place amongst some boulders, and so we curled up around them and hoped for the best.

The planes, fortunately for us, selected the obvious target. They swooped low and dropped their bombs on the ruined walls of the castle up on top of the hill. When the dust settled, and we crawled out of our hiding place, we saw that the hill no longer had a ruined castle on the top, it had simply been blown away. I looked at Walt. He just raised his eyebrows slightly but said nothing.

We moved on quickly after that. There was no point in staying still now that the enemy had found us. The planes would just return time and time again. The Rebels owned the sky. I hadn't seen a single Republican plane yet. The others said there were some, but they were vastly outnumbered.

That was the day that the winter ended, and spring arrived. As the hours slipped by, the temperature steadily increased until, come mid-afternoon, we were drenched in sweat and just trudging wearily onward, heads bowed. My stomach was twisting itself in knots, begging for food, moaning and groaning like a dying cat. My water bottle was empty, so was Jacks', and Walt didn't have any more of his horrible coñac.

We found some relief at dusk, a small mountain stream, fast-flowing and fresh. We rushed towards it and stuck our sun-burned lips into its delightful coolness. We stripped off our shirts and washed the grime off our torsos and then dunked our heads under the surface to clean the dust out of our hair.

Finally, we sat at the side of the stream letting the water trickle over our feet. My feet were aching and sore, but there were others who were in a worse situation. Not everyone had nice British boots like jack and I. The Spanish issue boots seemed to be made of cardboard, and there were some who only had shoes with soles made of rope which were called alpargatas.

The terrain was loose stone and shale mostly, goat tracks leading through the hills. There was little shelter from the relentless sun. The occasional gnarled olive tree, a few bushes and plenty of coarse grass. There were boulders strewn around and plenty of large red rocks to sit on.

As it was getting dark, it was felt safe enough to stop for the night. We looked around for somewhere to curl up, a little hollow or a gap between boulders. It might have been baking hot throughout the long afternoon, but none of us doubted that come the darkness the temperature would drop. I wrapped myself in my blanket and lay on some rough grass with jack beside me. Just before I fell into an exhausted sleep, I realised I had survived another day.

I was awoken in the early hours and told to keep watch for a while. I had a quick drink of water, but what I would really have liked would have been some food. It was my moaning stomach and the thunderous snores of my sleeping comrades that kept me company through that part of the night. When at last I was relieved by Jack, I stumbled back to my place and quickly fell asleep once more.

*

We were up before dawn and on our way just as the sun began to reach over the distant mountains. The air was cool, and I breathed it in deeply. It was going to be another long hot day. I hoped we would get wherever it was that we were supposed to be going. If I didn't get something to eat, I was likely to drop dead from exhaustion.

We hadn't been walking too long when we came to a road. It was obvious that the Republican army had passed this way. The roadside was littered with discarded items: empty ammunition boxes, the odd rifle, stray items of winter clothing. Although it was dangerous to be on a road, we were told we would take the risk and try to catch up to the rear of our retreating army. We needed food and ammunition and of course we needed leadership and the chance to find out the bigger picture.

We came to a bend in the road where we found bodies riddled with bullet holes. The ground was cut up all around. The column of Republicans had obviously been attacked by planes the previous day. There were flies everywhere and crows picking at the corpses. We pulled the bodies off the road and into a ditch and then moved on. We walked as quickly as we could, scurrying like rats along the dusty road. If we could catch up with the main body of our army it would be a great relief.

A bit further on, we came across an abandoned lorry. It must have run out of petrol. I was told to climb up into the back to see if there was anything worthwhile in there. Not surprisingly, there was nothing of any use. I would have liked to have found some tins of sardines or even just a half sack of stale bread, but there was nothing.

The sun was high in the sky when at last we saw the stragglers of the army up ahead. These were the walking wounded or the dead exhausted, those who just couldn't keep up with the pace of the main group. We passed through them. Some saw us and decided to give an extra effort and keep up with us to re-join their comrades, some didn't even acknowledge us. One tried to get in with our group, but just toppled off the road into the ditch to die.

An hour later, we caught up with the main body of our Brigade. A halt was immediately called, and we fell by the roadside. We drank from our water bottles whilst we waited for something to eat. Soon a couple of donkeys were led over to us and we huddled around them clutching our mess tins waiting for the cook to ladle us out our share.

It was some sort of vegetable broth, obviously cold as it had been made the day before and there was no way they were going to light fires to heat it up for us. It also looked like it had been watered down to make it go farther, but it didn't matter, we consumed it in seconds and begged for more.

Walt told me to check to see if there was a lorry with ammunition for our machinegun. If there wasn't maybe he would ditch it, he was exhausted from having to carry it. We had ditched almost everything that wasn't essential. Even our thick coats had been left in Belchite, although that had not been on purpose, but rather in our rush to get out of the house that was going to be destroyed. But I was glad not to have to carry it as the days were so hot. At night, it was a different story of course, sleeping in the open under a thin blanket was when I really missed my coat.

I found a lorry with ammunition for our French machinegun, not Russian machinegun ammunition this time. I took it all, even though there was no way I could possibly carry it by myself. I figured Walt would get some of the others to help. If I left it in the lorry it would just be blown up when the Rebel planes found us, which of course they would. I struggled back to the others loaded down with machinegun belts and carrying a wooden box of rifle ammunition.

Then we were on the move again. There was no point in sitting still, we had to retreat to somewhere that was still worth defending, somewhere where we could be reinforced. Out in open country we were sitting ducks for aeroplanes.

Word was passed around that we were heading for the village of Lécera wherever that might be. I just hoped that it was close and that we would find good defensive positions there, better than we had had in Belchite.

Moving slowly in a long column along the road we were sitting ducks for planes. We all watched the sky as we shuffled along. The sky was clear and blue, nothing like an English sky. I don't think I had ever seen a sky so devoid of clouds. There wasn't even a hint of white, not even way up high where it would be hardly visible. Great weather for planes. Visibility must be miles. The good thing was that if we were vigilant enough, we would see them coming from a long way off. But they would be able to take out the few lorries we had with us, and that would be the end of our basic supplies. It was essential that we reached Lécera as soon as possible.

CHAPTER FIVE

We were lucky, no aircraft found us on that long hot afternoon. However, when we finally got close enough to see Lécera through a gap in the hills, we realised that the planes had been busy dropping their bombs there instead of on us. Smoke was drifting upwards from several burning buildings and lorries and troops were milling around everywhere, and they weren't ours.

Standing out, tall and proud, was the spire of the Mudejar church, so typical of the little Aragonese villages that we were to pass through or around that vicious spring. It was constructed of thin red-brown bricks, obviously made from the earth around. And it leaned ever so slightly, as they all seemed to. But there it stood, towering above a ragged collection of squat houses. The bells were ringing out loud and clear, sounding out the entry of the Nationalists into yet another former Republican village. I thought they sounded a little sad, and maybe they were. One could only imagine what might be happening in that place at that moment. Republican supporters would be chased through the streets and taken to the main square to be shot. I'd been told that that was what normally happened. Anyone who had the means would have fled before the enemy's arrival, but those who had been left behind would not be shown any mercy: the elderly, the infirm, young war widows with a gaggle of starving children, the pig-headed and the insane.

"They shoots foreigners," Walt whispered in my ear. "Any foreigners what came to fight in Spain are shot if they gets captured. An' they 'ates machinegunners above all."

I wasn't sure whether to believe him or not, maybe he was just trying to scare me so that I wouldn't desert to the enemy at the earliest opportunity. I was, after all, of very dubious political persuasion. But I decided then and there not to be taken prisoner. I would die fighting rather than be captured.

We left the road and bypassed Lécera, leaving it in its ageless hollow between the low hills of the Campo de Belchite. Leaving it to its fate at the butchering hands of the Fascists. There was nothing we could do but head on towards the next village and hope that it was still holding out.

It was passed along the line that the next place we were aiming for was Hijar, some twenty kilometres away. It was probably more, as we were now heading across country. As it was late afternoon, we removed what we thought might be useful from the lorries and abandoned them. We loaded up the few remaining donkeys before setting off to put some distance between ourselves and the road.

Once we had gone a few kilometres, we came to a dip in the ground bordered by low hedges and a few stunted trees, and there we settled for the night. Fires were started, as it was thought that they wouldn't easily be spotted as we were nestled down low in the terrain. Besides, after a hard day of retreating and the disappointment of finding Lécera already in the hands of the Rebels, we needed something warm in our stomachs. It would lift our spirits ready for the next day, which was going to be another difficult one.

Lentils were boiled up and we ate our small share in silence sitting round the fire. After I left Spain, I could never touch any of the foods that they had given us there. Lentils, chickpeas, all the various kinds of beans. Legumbres they were called, lumping them all together into one desperate food group. They were the staple diet of the Republican Zone during the war. Was it any better for the other side? Probably not, but we couldn't help but imagine them having lorries loaded with fresh-baked bread, cured hams, goats' cheese and salted cod. All you could eat and more. Our near-starvation diet did terrible things to the mind.

Food was one of the main topics of conversation as we readied ourselves for the night. Some remembered a mother's apple pie, others a magnificent Sunday roast with thick, steaming gravy. I longed for the frugal meals of our former landlady which now seemed like royal banquets.

Gradually, as the fire died down, so did the talk, and the men shut themselves off from their current situation and thought about home for a while. A sweetheart, a wife and children, some girl they had loved from a distance but never dared to speak to. I had no one, but I did miss England. I did miss England, lying there on the hard ground of the war-torn fields of Aragon. I missed the hustle and bustle of the building site, a sudden shower of rain, the smell of steak and kidney pie. And with those thoughts, I would quickly fall asleep. If I was lucky, I would have a couple of hours before being called for sentry duty.

*

I was awoken not long before dawn to take the last watch. Some of the men were already half-awake, coughing quietly and cursing the lack of cigarettes or taking a quick drink of water to clear a headache before trying to snatch that last blissful half an hour of rest. I should have been woken up long before, but the sentries that night must have fallen asleep. It was easy to do. I walked up a slope away from the main group and lay down at the top of the ridge. I peered off across the desolate landscape back the way we had come. I could hear the forlorn hoot of a distant owl, desperate to find something to eat before sunrise. It might have been a long night of hunting and finding nothing. It was strange how normal things were continuing, despite the war that was raging all around. This little pocket of Spain, with its red earth, bleached trees and cowering villages, had unwittingly become the focal point of the whole damn war. Maybe of the whole damn world.

Jack came up the slope to find me with a small hunk of bread. He tore it into two and gave me my share.

"Look at us Billy, we're soldiers," he said. There seemed some hint of pride in his voice.

"We're idiots," I responded and choked as the granite bread stuck in my throat. Jack slapped me on the back and the chunk that I had been chewing returned to my mouth.

"Here," he said laughing, handing me his water bottle, "you need to wet it a bit, make it softer. Be easier to swallow."

I did as he said and managed to get it all down. Who knew when we might next be able to eat?

As soon as it was light, we were moving. Men complained of aching muscles. Walt said his back hurt from carrying the machinegun, but no one was about to offer to carry it for him. That gun was his personal cross, anyone else would have ditched it long ago. And his stubbornness meant that Jack had to carry the tripod and I had to carry ammunition belts slung all over my body, three others carried them too. They got heavier and heavier as the day's march continued. Walt thought the gun would ultimately save us. He was convinced about it. I wasn't so sure. Jack thought the whole idea was stupid and told Walt so at every opportunity. Going up each slope was murder.

After a couple of hours of undulating hills, climbing over ruined stone walls and tripping over rocks, we found an old abandoned olive grove beside a narrow dirt-track road that snaked a way off through the hills.

We were told to rest, whilst a decision was made as to whether the road was the right way to go. A handful of men were sent towards the top of the nearest hill to scout out the lie of the land. They hadn't got more than halfway up, when a group of Rebels suddenly came over the top of the hill. Our men turned to run back towards the main group. The Fascists opened fire. One of the men, running as fast as he could downhill, tripped and fell. As he tried to stand up, a bullet ripped into his throat and he fell back down as if in slow motion. Another was hit in the back and seemed to cartwheel down the slope.

As one, we took to our feet. We raced towards the far side of the olive grove and clambered over the low stone wall. Once on the other side of the road we were off across country, running for our lives. We didn't know just how many Fascists were about to pour over that hill, and we didn't want to hang around to find out. Shots rang out and soon enough there was the familiar bark of a machinegun and then a second one. Any stragglers were cut down amongst the olive trees or slaughtered as they tried to cross the road.

I paused for a second to look behind me. The enemy wasn't running after us. Instead, they were firing endlessly from the top of the hill down into the olive grove. Walt was struggling with the heavy machinegun in both hands. Jack came back to me.

"We've got to 'elp 'im," he decided. We reached Walt and grabbed the gun off him. Jack gave him the tripod and then we were running once more, uphill, Jack and I carrying the gun between us.

We didn't stop running when we were over the first hill, but we ran out of steam halfway up the second one. We just managed to plod on to the summit and then we dropped down, exhausted.

*

We weren't given long to recover, just enough time to get some air into our lungs, and then we were on our feet once more. I took a quick gulp from my water bottle, but not much, I had no idea when I might be able to refill it. The donkeys had been left behind in the olive grove in our panic to get away. That meant no food or extra ammunition. What we carried with us was all that we had. We would have to hope that Hijar was still in Republican hands and that there were supplies there. It was obvious that the Rebels were right on our heels. It was a race to see who would reach Hijar first. They of course could use the road, but we could not. Perhaps their planes were already bombing the place, and we would get there only to find it already destroyed.

Hijar took on a huge significance for me, as if it were the end of some great and worthy adventure. Its streets would be covered in flowers, the women would blow down kisses from their balconies and the main square would have a huge fountain of icy mountain water, where we could bathe and cool our feet. In the evenings, whilst the young men played guitars and their girls danced for us, we would feast on *ternasco* and wild mushrooms. Perhaps the heat was driving me crazy, I don't remember. But, this image of Hijar as some sort of small heaven kept me going. It kept me putting one foot in front of the other, always staring at my feet, never looking ahead to the next stunted hill that needed to be climbed.

We rested in the brief shade of a rocky outcrop around midday. All the time, stragglers arrived, tripping in, in groups of two or three, limping, helping each other, desperate not to be left behind for the Fascists to find. We couldn't wait for long. We got to our feet again after the briefest of pauses, Walt looked sadly at Jack and I.

"We've gotta lose the gun," he said, head bowed. "We ain't gonna make it if we 'ave to lug that thing with us."

He was right. We had been struggling at the back of the main group. If we continued to haul the gun we would fall behind for sure. To keep the machinegun was suicide. We left it hidden under some stones beneath a dwarf bush. As we walked away, Jack threw the tripod into a gully and I gradually let my ammunition belts slip to the floor as we walked. Seeing what I was doing, the others who had been carrying spare belts did the same. It was a great relief not to be weighed down by them. They had made me sweat and their roughness had scraped at the skin beneath my thin shirt. It was as if I had been given a new lease of life, and I felt a freedom of movement that almost made me want to run on ahead of the group.

I wondered if anything would happen to us for losing our machinegun, but it was more than likely that the person who had given it to us was already dead. It seemed such a long time ago when the lorries loaded with weapons had reached Talavera de la Mancha. What I wouldn't have given to have been back there in the middle of a snowstorm in that leaking barracks with only the warmth of a half plate of vegetable broth to look forward to.

I expected us to stop for the night. I certainly hadn't been saving any energy to keep going beyond sunset, especially after a day with no food. But we were in very real danger of being outflanked and cut off behind enemy lines. We had to keep moving. Our only hope was to reach Hijar before it fell to the Rebels. Maybe there might be lorries there that could take us to safety in Catalunya. I was certainly fed up with walking across the Aragon.

After a brief stop just before it got dark, we were underway again. Some men cursed but most saved their breath, knowing that there was no other choice. A few just remained sprawled on the ground. They gave up. Nobody made a move to bully them back onto their feet, it was everyman for himself. Those who preferred to die alone on a desolate hillside could do so. Some might be picked up by enemy scouts who were probably following us, some might be food for wolves said Walt. I wasn't a hundred percent sure about the wolves theory. I certainly hadn't heard any howling at night. Maybe Walt was trying to wind me up, or motivate me to keep going.

We hadn't gone far, when a lone shot rang out. Someone had used a bullet to put an end to his suffering. You couldn't really blame him. We were exhausted beyond the limits of human endurance. We had had no food and little water. We were zombies just trudging ever onwards. And now we had a night march ahead of us.

CHAPTER SIX

By the light of a waning moon, we moved on. The sky changed from purple to black. The clouds dropped lower and pressed down upon us, wanting to push us into the ground, so that our feet dragged more than ever.

At different stages during that difficult night, we came across small groups of our own soldiers or civilians. A family, complete with grandparents, all huddled together beneath a stunted tree watched us pass like ghosts and said nothing. Some of the soldiers picked themselves up and joined our slow-moving column. They were probably deserters who had fled from the fighting around Belchite or Lécera, but nothing was said. They picked themselves up and just stumbled along beside us, happy to be part of a large group once more.

As the night wore on, our ragtag force swelled as civilians decided to follow us to safety. They had no idea what was happening in the war, all they knew was that we were on their side, and soldiers with guns meant protection. At least it must have seemed like that to them. The truth was different, we were just as exhausted and scared as they were. There were mothers with babies in their arms, babies that had long ago given up crying. There were old men and women shuffling in silence maybe wearing just slippers on their feet. I didn't think they would keep pace with us for long. On the ground beside the goat track we were following through the hills, was the flotsam and jetsam of a thousand shattered lives. People had started out carrying their most prized possessions, but when they realised that they were being slowed down, they had started to throw away anything that wasn't essential. Just as we had done with our machinegun. The track was lined with discarded clothing, pots and pans, empty earthenware jugs. We even saw a straw mattress and Jack threw himself down on it to have a minute's rest. He got up declaring that he felt better than ever.

We came across a paper bag that contained money. The bag had split open when it had been dumped and the notes were lazily blowing with the pre-dawn breeze. I bent down and picked up a couple of the pieces of printed paper. They had been issued by the Colectividad Libre of Lécera. One was of the value of twenty-five céntimos, the other was for one peseta. Now that the cooperative no longer existed, they were worthless. I stuffed them into my shirt pocket as a souvenir.

Some people begged us for food or just repeated *agua* at us. We had nothing to spare. Some of the civilians who were more determined managed to stay with us for a few kilometres before eventually giving up. We picked up new ones to replace them. It was obvious that the Republic at least on this front was in total chaos.

I took a sip of water as we stopped just as the sun was rising above the distant mountains. The peaks were snow-bound, and I would have loved to have been able to start at a summit and roll myself down it through the snow. I would fill my boots with snow to relieve the burning of my feet and rub snow all over my face and in my hair. Although the temperature had dropped during the night, the fact that we had been constantly on the move meant that my body had never stopped sweating. The dust that swirled about as we walked stuck to our clothes and our faces. You could feel it in your nose and mouth and ears.

We sat on some boulders by the side of the track and removed our boots. I took off my sweaty socks and changed them for another pair. They weren't clean socks, but they were dry. Walt was picking at his blisters and complaining about the boots he had been issued which were too small for him. Walt was such a big man, that they probably didn't make stuff in his size in Spain. His uniform seemed to have been stitched together from different items to make things big enough for him. His brown corduroy trousers swung above his ankles and his army tunic couldn't be buttoned up because his chest was too wide. He had on an undershirt which he must have brought with him from home and which might once have been white but was now a dirty brown. Even the sweat-soaked and sun-bleached beret on his head was way too small.

Before we set off again, I changed my shirt. As with the socks, it wasn't a clean shirt, just drier than the one I had been wearing. I would have liked a nice cold bath, to sink my sunburnt face beneath the water and let it cool there for hours. Funny how the things I most used to take for granted were the things I missed the most – water for a bath and to drink, something to eat when I wanted it, a roof over my head, a mattress to sleep on at night to ease the permanent ache in my joints.

We were so exhausted, that we were no longer as vigilant as we should have been. No one was scanning the sky as we had been the previous day. So, it was no surprise that the first sign of approaching enemy planes, was the sound of their engines almost directly overhead. They had appeared over the top a hill without warning. Those of us who were soldiers recognised the noise and set off running to try to find some cover. The civilians were unsure of what action to take and most stood looking up at the planes as they raced towards them, hands shielding their eyes from the brightness of the sun. A few, seeing us fleeing for our lives decided to do the same, but those who remained on the path in frozen inactivity had no chance. There would be some who had never seen an aircraft before. The planes tore along the length of the track, their guns barking.

It was chaos. People were running, falling, picking themselves up, falling again. Then, as the planes got nearer, we heard the whistle of their bombs and the ground shook and the whole world seemed to explode in upon us.

Jack and I had made it further away across the fields than most and we flung ourselves down and stayed still. Walt was bigger and slower and seemed to be running through a hail of bullets that tore up the ground all around him like raindrops on a puddle. I thought it impossible that he would survive, but somehow, he wasn't hit, and the plane that had been targeting him had to pull up. At last he reached us and threw himself down, hands over his head, panting like a dog. I'd never seen the big man look so scared.

We watched the planes lazily turn and head back to their airfield, which was probably in Zaragoza. Whilst much of the Aragon had been in Republican hands since the beginning of the war, the three largest cities had fallen to the Fascists. And it was from Zaragoza that the Rebels had mounted their push towards the Mediterranean.

As the noise of the planes slowly receded, it was replaced by human sounds. The screams of the wounded. The cries of mothers looking for their children. The useless shouting of some of the soldiers who were shaking their fists in anger at the disappearing enemy. There was nothing we could have done. We hadn't even bothered to waste ammunition by firing off a few shots.

We left the scene straightaway, there was no point in staying there. Any delay might mean that we were outflanked by the enemy's ground troops. It was vitally important that we reached Hijar before the Nationalists. We needed to rest, we needed to eat, and we needed somewhere to feel safe. For those reasons we had no choice but to press on.

We trudged onward and soon the wailing of the people who had been fleeing with us died away as we abandoned them to their grief. Perhaps they would be safer without us. We couldn't wait for them or carry their wounded children, we had to keep going.

The sun showed no mercy throughout the endless hours of the afternoon. People were starting to flag. The column was now moving at a snail's pace. I think even the most optimistic amongst us would have realised that the Rebels would reach Hijar long before us. They would have lorries to get them there via the most direct route. Then they would be rested and fed, waiting for us. They would have air support to tell them when we were close. They would have field guns and machineguns and an endless supply of ammunition. Hijar no longer seemed like some small heaven, rather some terrible hell. A badly disguised trap just waiting for us to fall into.

CHAPTER SEVEN

That night we had to stop to rest. We were dead on our feet. Had we tried to continue, none of us would have reached Hijar. The likelihood was that when we reached the village, we would instantly be thrown into battle. We couldn't hope to win a battle after walking across country for two days and two nights almost without stopping.

I was given the first watch this time, along with an older Spaniard. It was thought that with two of us together we might stay awake. My companion was stocky and robust with a bushy black beard. His skin was the same colour as the earth and his eyes were black like coal. He tried to make conversation with me, but apart from *agua* I had no Spanish at all, and of course he had no English. We both drifted off into our own thoughts and soon I heard him snoring softly. I managed to stay awake, despite my exhaustion. I was terrified that Franco's dreaded Moroccan Army might creep up on us during the darkness. I had heard that they ate young brigadistas like me for breakfast.

When Jack came to relieve me, I found a little bush and curled up under it. I wrapped my blanket tightly around me as the temperature would drop in the hours towards morning. It seemed like only a few minutes before Walt was kicking my boot to wake me up.

"Come on, lazy arse. Time to get moving."
"What's for breakfast?" I mumbled.
"What would Sir like? Full English?"
Within no time, we were on the move once more. Everyone seemed stiff and sore and hobbled for the first hour or so, but after that, we seemed to get back into our trancelike groove, just putting one foot in front of the other, not looking ahead, just walking. Occasionally, someone would stumble on a rock and fall down cursing. Others, without warning, just keeled over onto the grass beside the track. Just a short rest they would say. They would catch us up soon enough. If they had friends, then they would be lifted back onto their feet and supported for a while until they got back into the rhythm required to keep moving despite everything. If they didn't, then they could rest all they wanted.

How much further could it be? The sun was climbing ever higher. It was going to be another long hot, dusty day. I took a tiny sip of water when my throat had become so dry that I could no longer swallow. My tongue was starting to swell. All the while, my stomach growled, twisting itself into knots. I'd been hungry all my life, there had never been a single occasion when I had eaten enough to feel full, but I had never experienced hunger pains like now. But this wasn't just hunger, it was slow, agonising death by starvation. I recalled my grandmother when I was a child and how she would go days without food so that I might have her share. She never once complained. I took it for granted at the time that she just didn't feel hungry or didn't need to eat everyday like I did. Now I knew how she must have felt. I realised, too late of course, the sacrifice she had made for me. I felt disappointed with myself for not having insisted that she eat her share.

Suddenly, after another hour or so, our long and winding column came to a halt. Someone from the Brigade had found us. God only knew how. For all I could tell we were in the middle of nowhere. Of course, by this stage, we weren't just our brigade. We were a mixture of all the brigades who had been thrown into the breach made all along the Aragon Front.

The news was not good. Hijar had fallen to the Rebels after a dawn attack and had been abandoned. The Republic was on the verge of collapse. We were now going to head for a place called Alcañiz. It was the largest town in that part of the Aragon and had a formidable castle on top of a robust hill. It was thought to be a good defensive position. I remembered what had happened to the last castle we had attempted to defend. If we weren't provided with air cover, then we were sitting ducks wherever we went. I just hoped there would be food there and a fountain to drink from and wash in. A lorry-load of new uniforms would be nice too, my clothes were like filthy rags and stiff as cardboard.

So, we left Hijar behind us. At least we hadn't walked into the trap. But we hadn't had the chance to rest or to get any food either. It was like running a bloody marathon, only to reach the finish line to be told that the race wasn't over, and you had to run the whole damn thing over again. There was no guarantee that Alcañiz wouldn't fall to the Rebels too before we got there, they were moving a lot faster than we were. We didn't know what their objective was, how could we? Our only hope was that their lightning advance would come to a halt. It was possible that Franco thought that now was the moment to finish the war. He had the Republic on the run, and maybe he wouldn't stop until we were chased into the Mediterranean. The end of the legitimate government of Spain could be in sight. It was a sobering thought.

*

In the afternoon, we came across a small wood at the base of a hill where a little stream ran. At last, we were able to bathe and wash our clothes and of course to get a drink and refill our parched water bottles. I dunked my burning face into the water which was breathtakingly cold as it came from melting snow from the nearby mountains. We were walking into an area called the Desierto de Calanda. If it really was a desert, then it might be quite a while before we found another stream like this one. We had now left the province of Zaragoza and crossed into the province of Teruel. The very mention reminded everyone of the winter defeat in the city of the same name.

In the distance, we could see two mountains which we would have to pass between on the way to Alcañiz. It would be easy for the enemy to trap us there. If they knew how exhausted we were, if they knew how limited our ammunition supply was, then they would hit us with everything they had. The battle for the Aragon could be all over in a matter of hours. Our only hope, was that we might somehow get ahead of the Rebels and find some place to halt their advance.

Perhaps our leaders might come up with a plan for a surprise attack along another sector to relieve the pressure on us. But the Republic seemed to be on its last legs. There wouldn't be planes or tanks or artillery for a big push somewhere else. If there had been, then they would have been rushed to the Aragon Sector to help us defend this vital area that was the link between Catalunya and the Madrid-Valencia corridor.

Now that we had contact with the Brigade, we hoped that we might be provided with food and supplies. It would be difficult, since we were lost in the hills, and the supply base of Hijar had also been lost. Anything that came would have to be brought from Alcañiz, but we had to hope that that was possible.

In the afternoon, we were found by a Spanish captain. Eventually, with a little help from gestures and signs he managed to communicate that a group of us should press on ahead and climb to the high ground. That would stop the main group from walking into a trap. It was the sensible thing to do of course.

Walt took charge of getting a group together. Not surprisingly, he selected Jack and I to go with him. I was pleased that over the course of just a few days, he now viewed us not as boys but as fellow soldiers. We had repeatedly faced death together, and now we were going to do it again. If the Fascists were going to attack us, they would want to control the high ground.

CHAPTER EIGHT

We left the rest of the column and pushed on ahead. Yes, we were fatigued, but we had a mission to undertake and we were keen to get on with it. We were to reach the high ground that had been indicated to us, hold it against any enemy attacks and then wait there until the whole column had passed through the gap. Then, we would have to catch back up to the rear and head on towards Alcañiz. If the brigade headquarters were there, there had to be a hope that the defenders would do anything necessary to hold out. Having said that, I knew from first-hand experience what an air bombardment could do. We had seen back in Belchite just how quickly the Rebels could overrun a town with their air domination and superior artillery.

It was hard work climbing up the steep slope, perhaps we were expecting too much of bodies that were dangerously short of energy. It seemed to take forever to clamber our way to the summit, tripping over loose stones as we went, clutching at clumps of dry grass with our hands.

Walt was the first one to reach the top of the hill. Without the machine gun to weigh him down, he was proving capable of super-human feats. I just wondered how much longer a body like his could survive on a starvation diet. Me, I was just skin and bones. A bundle of twigs wrapped in an over-sized uniform, but Walt? Walt was at least three of me put together. And his personality was as big as his body. To me he seemed indestructible. Not only his body but his mind. I don't think either Jack or myself would have survived those terrible days without him. He moaned about being our babysitter, but I like to think there was a little part of him that was grateful for having us around. Maybe we just allowed him to take his mind off other things for a bit. He teased us at times. Bullied us not to give up. Whatever needed to be done. I think if he had ever had children, he would have been a great dad. I could imagine him carrying a child up on his shoulders for hours and never tiring. It would be like riding an elephant.

As he reached the crest of the hill, the big man suddenly threw himself to the ground. He made hurried signals for us to be quiet and to keep low. When at last we had all reached him, he explained in a hushed voice that there were thirty or forty Fascists sitting on the downslope.

"What are they doing?" whispered Jack.

"Looks like they're takin' a breather," replied Walt.

"What we gonna do?" I asked.

"Let's kill the bastards," decided Walt.

"They outnumber us," someone pointed out to him.

"And we're knackered," wheezed someone else.

"Fuck it!" said Walt. "We came 'ere to kill Fascists and that's what we're gonna do."

"I'm with you," said Jack.

"Me too," I added quickly, not that my participation would be of any importance.

"What about the rest of ya?" asked Walt, his voice a venomous hiss. "If these two kids are man enough, what 'bout you lot?"

There was a general nodding of heads.

"We don't have any grenades," put in someone.

Walt looked around him and bent and picked up a small rock.

"They don't know we ain't got any grenades," he whispered. The rest of us quickly searched around for good-sized rocks. When we were ready, we gathered just below the top of the rise and waited for Walt to give the word. I don't remember being scared. I think we had spent so much time being harassed by the enemy from a distance that we were relieved to be able to fight back at last.

"Now!" shouted Walt, and screaming like a banshee, he leapt to his feet and disappeared over the summit of the hill. The rest of us were right after him. We all screamed things like 'death to the Fascists' or 'kill the Fascist swine.' And then we were throwing our rocks at the startled Rebels. They had been so sure of themselves, that they hadn't even bothered to post sentries. Some of them were lying as if asleep, others sitting and smoking. Our unexpected charge threw them into a terrible panic.

"Rojos!" I heard one of them shout in alarm. And then all sound was drowned out except for the sound of gunfire. I brought my rifle up to my shoulder, screwed one eye shut, looked along the barrel at the sight, thought I saw a target and fired. As soon as the bullet was on its way I was firing again. It only took a matter of minutes, although it seemed like forever, and it was all over. About ten Fascists lay dead, the rest were running. Tripping, falling, cursing us as Red Devils, they charged back down the slope in the direction they had come from in a total panic. For all they knew, the whole Republican Army of the Aragon was about to come over the crest of their hill, march down into the valley and retake Hijar.

We stood on the top of that desolate peak and shouted abuse after them. It was a brief illusion of victory in a never-ending saga of defeat. We milked the feeling of euphoria for all we could. Who knew when we would get to feel like that again?

When eventually the adrenalin had died away and our heartrates had returned to normal, we set about picking over the bodies of the Fascists and taking anything that was edible or smokable or drinkable. We found a few grenades and although their rifles looked infinitely better that ours, we didn't take them because we would never be able to get ammunition for them in the long term.

We placed all the food items together in a pile. There wasn't that much, they had obviously been expecting to be fed that day, but there were a few tins of sardines, some small chorizos and pieces of cheese as hard as stone. There were chunks of bread too, old and stale, but better that any bread ever made on our side. Walt found a couple of bottles of coñac and there were several sacks of wine. I found a water bottle and took a quick drink before anyone else saw me.

The last man that we checked suddenly moaned causing us all to freeze. The bastard was still alive. We knew that the Fascists didn't like to take prisoners. They tended to just shoot them on the spot. It was rumoured that they had a special loathing for Brigadistas like us. We knew that if we fell into the enemy's hands, then no mercy would be shown. And here was one of them. This man would have shot us like dogs given half the chance. He was lying against a jagged rock bleeding from a bullet wound to the chest. It looked like he might bleed to death. We clustered around him. No one quite knew what to do. After a while, his eyes fluttered open, and upon seeing us all staring down at him, a sudden panic gripped him. You could see the terror in his eyes. He tried to twist himself around in order to get up, but he was too weak and just fell back sobbing. He had to assume we would shoot him. After all, that was what he would have done to any of us had the situation been reversed.

"Shoot 'im," said Walt to me.

"I can't do it Walt," I told him, dropping back from the crowd.

"I'll do it," came Jack's voice.

"Good lad!" said Walt.

"Don't do it Jack," I whispered at him, but I knew his mind was already made up. Jack wanted to show himself to be as big and strong as Walt and the other veterans, this was his chance to prove that he could be ruthless when needed.

I turned away. I heard the Fascist begging Jack although I didn't know what his exact words meant. And then there was a shot. When I turned back, I saw that the man's face had been blown away.

"Good lad," said Walt, patting Jack on the back.

*

The top of the ridge was a lonely and desolate place. There were no trees and no large boulders to give us cover either from the enemy or from the blazing sun. Throughout the long afternoon, we walked slowly as our column advanced through the valley below. It was strung out and winding like the river which must once have carved a way through this area, but which had long ago dried up.

A few enemy planes could have swooped down and wiped out half the Army of the Aragon in a matter of minutes. There was nowhere to hide down in that dried river-bed valley. I could only conclude that the Rebels were more intent on capturing towns and villages. They would stop for a rest in each new place and right a few wrongs while they were there. Then they would move on once more, fully fed and bathed and ready for more easy conquests on their never-ending route of glorious victories. You could imagine the Fascist newspapers screaming out headlines with little Aragonese villages as their titles, imaging them as being of huge strategic importance. In reality, they were nothing more than little hamlets made up of rundown houses, clustered around a once beautiful church. The churches in Republican Spain had suffered greatly as the people had turned against the religion of their ancestors. Priests along with other presumed intellectuals were shot and their churches desecrated and burned. Often only the tall spires remained intact, like imploring fingers pointing up towards a heaven that, at least on the Republican side, had ceased to exist.

The Fascists would enter these long-forgotten villages. Restore the old order and the old religion, shoot the leaders of the local cooperative and any sindicalistas and then leave. Those who had been secret Nationalist sympathisers, or those who felt they had been wronged by the legitimate government, would then seize the opportunity to become someone they could only have dreamed of becoming. Reprisals were plentiful and the settling of family feuds and personal grievances abounded. There was no law in these places once the soldiers had marched away, the cruelty of human nature ruled, totally unchecked.

*

Towards dusk, just below us on the Fascist side of the ridge, we saw a little abandoned farmhouse. It was typical of this area. A family had tried to survive off the land and built themselves a small house with a few outbuildings for livestock Then they had been forced to abandon it, probably as a result of continuous poor harvests because of the chronic shortage of water. What had possessed them to try in the first place? I couldn't really imagine a worse place to try to farm, although of course I was a city boy and knew nothing about making a living from the land. The winters would be freezing, and the hills would be deep in snow, and the summers would be parched and suffocating. The wind would have driven them mad night after lonely night.

A few stunted trees remained within the stepped terraces of the smallholding. They were, according to one of the men who had spent a while in Spain, just olives, almonds and cherries, the only trees that could live in near drought conditions. But as we neared the farm with the intention of spending the night, we saw that even these hardy species had been unable to survive. The few leaves that remained on the olive trees were dry and curled, and the almonds and cherries were just dried sticks stuck into the uncaring earth. The soil was a red powder and it was impossible to imagine that anything worthwhile would ever grow there.

Walt went into the farmhouse to inspect it, but not surprisingly there was nothing of any use. We couldn't even use it as a shelter to spend the night since the tiled roof had long ago collapsed in upon itself after generations of mountain storms. The floor was a mass of shattered tiles and broken beams. Instead, we lay about under the decimated trees and shared out the last of the Fascist food. I remember taking a bite of chorizo and thinking it was the best thing I had ever tasted. We washed it down with wine and then drank coñac into the night, just little sips as the bottles were passed around. We didn't post sentries as we were past caring.

CHAPTER NINE

At some time during the night, a cruel wind picked up and screamed along the valley and up and over the hills. I huddled beneath my threadbare blanket and shivered and longed for home. I couldn't help but imagine the poor family that had once lived there. What must it have been like to suffer this terrible wind night after night? The Spanish soldiers who had lived locally referred to it as the cierzo. It was said at times to reach such speeds as to be able to blow a man clean off his feet. It meant that we spent a wretched night as this evil wind howled right through us. It was like the Grim Reaper's evil brother had come to visit.

Come the morning, and the cierzo had thankfully died away. We were soon up once more on our ridge and saw the last of the column down below us. They were lying about on the ground, reluctant to get up and start walking again. I could imagine that the wind had savaged them too, sticking its icy fingers down the necks of their tunics and up the legs of their trousers.

We began the downward trek into the valley below. It took a while. The slope was steep. We had to be careful of loose gravel and rocks, but it was easier going down than it had been climbing up.

When we finally reached the valley floor, we passed on through the men strewn around on the ground.

Some acknowledged us, most ignored us. The front of the column was just starting to get itself into order to continue the march. We reported to the captain who had sent us up to the high ground and explained to him as best we could that we had found some Fascists waiting there, and that we had driven them off back towards Hijar. Eventually, he seemed to understand, and he smiled.

"Hoy Alcañiz," he said triumphantly. He gave the order to move on, and with a collective groan, the men began the painful process of putting weight on feet that were covered in blisters or bleeding from cuts. Even my boots, which had been new not so long ago, were showing signs of wear and tear. I hoped that they would get me to Alcañiz. What a bedraggled spectacle we must have presented that forlorn morning. We looked nothing like an army, rather a beggars' outing gone astray.

We hadn't been walking long, hadn't really got over the initial stiffness, when we came to a small hamlet with a wooden bridge across a stream. There were a few abandoned houses and we instantly ransacked them in search of anything edible. Other soldiers or fleeing civilians had passed this way before us and left nothing. We waded into the stream with its freezing melt water and splashed it into our faces and dunked our heads in, to come out gasping for breath. We drank our fill and refilled our water bottles ready for another long, hot, dusty day. And then a miracle happened. A small group of men approached us leading a drove of emaciated donkeys.

They had been sent out from Alcañiz and they brought food and a little ammunition, although apparently there was a shortage in Alcañiz as well. There were sacks of bread and we each got half a small loaf and a half ladle of soup. I think if the donkeys had had any meat left on their bones then we might have butchered them and added them to our meal, but they were a sorry sight to see. In a worse state than we were. They passed back along the column, most of which still hadn't reached the stream where the front ranks were now enjoying breakfast.

It was heartening news that these men had been sent out from Alcañiz. It meant that the town was still in Loyalist hands. They were probably anxiously awaiting our arrival, terrified of facing the Fascists without us. Little did they know that we were hardly a fit fighting force anymore.

The Spanish captain decided to send the men back to Alcañiz with some of his troops to tell the town's commanders that we were on our way. I saw him looking at his little map, trying to work out just how long it might take us to arrive, but I couldn't understand his instructions to his men. They disappeared off with the villagers and their hobbling donkeys.

We weren't allowed to dawdle over breakfast, instead we were hurried on our way once more. I dipped my hand into the icy water and pulled a last handful up to my mouth. I was walking again. I felt the stiffness in my calves as a result of our descent from the hilltop and the familiar throbbing pain of my feet. I would have liked to have been able to wash my clothes in the stream, but there was no time. We had to reach Alcañiz before the Rebels did.

We walked into a new kind of landscape. The hills became lower and flat-topped as if they had been decapitated with a knife. The earth was light brown and the stones dark grey. In the distance there were taller hills topped with white clouds.

In the middle of some flat land between the hills, we came across what the local men referred to as a *masada*, a sort of luxury farm once owned by a rich family. They had plenty of land for their animals and would have had servants too. The whole place had been left to fall into disrepair. It was just a stark reminder of better days, days that were well and truly gone. Days that would surely never be known again.

In little over an hour, we were close enough to see a pall of dark smoke hanging over Alcañiz in the distance. We could see tiny black specs circling above it, like watching vultures. They were enemy aircraft. We could hear muffled explosions as bombs blew the houses apart. Occasionally, through a break in the smoke we might catch a glimpse of the castle, its walls shattered. It was more of a fine house than a defensive castle, with magnificent square towers. It sat upon a huge rock that dominated the village and seemed to have been levelled especially for the castle to be built on. The walls were the same colour as the rock upon which it stood. I thought it was sad to see it being blown to pieces. It must have watched over the town for centuries, but now, against modern weapons it was useless. The little houses clustered down below and to the righthand side were shrouded in smoke.

One member of the patrol that had been sent to Alcañiz returned, his eyes bloodshot and streaming, his hair on end like a madman. He had lost his rifle. Gasping for breath, he delivered his news.

There was a general groan from the Spanish troops when the captain told them, and we groaned too when one of our number with a little Spanish translated that Alcañiz had been abandoned and we were to head for Caspe. The captain studied his map for a while, took advice from a couple of his most trusted men and eventually pointed vaguely northwards and we set off once more. We gave Alcañiz a wide birth. Hopefully the Rebels wouldn't come looking for us too soon.

They must have bypassed us in the night on the main road to reach the town ahead of us. It was yet another disappointment along our journey of suffering. I was starting to wonder if we would ever find a place that was still in Republican hands.

*

We trudged on all day. It was roughly the same distance to Caspe as it had been from Hijar to Alcañiz, and we all knew how hard that journey had been. The terrain changed once more. Little hills like pimples dotted the landscape with, occasionally a huge grey outcrop as if it had just been dropped there from above. No one spoke, everyone was miserable and just longing for this terrible ordeal to be over. The sun pushed down on our heads and the loose earth tried to suck us in by our feet. We were doubling back on ourselves, back into the Province of Zaragoza. I had the sensation that we were just wandering around in circles without really going anywhere.

Occasionally, we would meet little groups of refugees who might ask where they could flee to escape from the Fascists. They would beg us for food and water. Some begged us to take their children with us. We ignored them and carried on climbing and then descending, always climbing or descending, there was rarely any flat country now. We looked for a stream or a lake but found no water all day. The vicious heat made us empty our water bottles and our throats became so dry that it was painful to swallow. And still we walked on. My rifle had begun to weigh me down. As the hours went by so its weight pulled ever harder on my shoulder. I would swap it from one to the other, but it made little difference. I was beginning to obsess that carrying it would kill me.

All of a sudden, I reached the end of my tether. I grabbed the rifle, snatched it off my shoulder and threw it as far away from me as possible. I just stood there, hands on my knees, bent forwards, gasping. The relief was immense.

"Billy you idiot," came Jack's voice. I looked up to see him heading off to retrieve my weapon. Being in such a weak state, I hadn't been able to throw it very far. He picked it up and brought it back to me.

"You can't fight without a rifle," he told me.

"My shoulders hurt," I mumbled wanting to burst into tears like a child.

"Then carry it out in front for a while," he said and showed me how to do it. I took his advice and carried the damn thing out in front at waist level until my arms ached and I was glad to get it back onto a shoulder.

The afternoon wore on, I glanced up at the sky in the hope of spotting a dark cloud which might bring the relief of rain, but there was nothing except a forever blue. There were no trees, just occasional low bushes, beaten down by the sun and bent double by the cierzo. On a distant mountain slope, we might see one of the little stone shelters. They had been built by shepherds so they could take refuge if they were caught by a sudden storm or if the cierzo blew out of control. It was a desolate place to have been alone looking after a small flock of sheep. I assumed that the shepherds must have ended up going completely mad. I think at that moment, in the state we were in, had we come across a flock of sheep we would have devoured them whole, wool and all. Perhaps shepherd and all.

*

I longed for nightfall and the chance to lie down and not have to continue plodding onwards. At last, when it got too dark to see the ground up ahead, we were told to halt. Within seconds every one of us collapsed. Some were pulling at their boots to find an annoying stone or relieve the cramp that had numbed their feet for so long, but most just lay still, gasping for breath. I had never felt so utterly done in. Even after a hard day on the building site lugging bricks up ladders to the tops of houses. I had never felt as wasted as this.

There was no food. There was no water. There was just the relief of being still at last. The relief of not having to keep climbing and descending. Eventually, we huddled into little groups, covered ourselves with our blankets and tried to sleep, despite our aching limbs and growling stomachs, and despite the hard stones we had to lie on.

*

At sunrise, we were ready to move on. The early morning was the best time for walking. On that day, there was even the illusion of a cooling breeze. It didn't stay long, chased away by the rising sun. It was going to be another hot one. We had no breakfast, and there was little hope of anything else to eat for the coming hours. There was also little hope of finding Caspe in Republican hands. Our great retreat was starting to follow a familiar pattern; hour upon hour of trudging through the hills only to find our destination already in the hands of the enemy. And then on once more, on towards the next little village and some imagined salvation. But, what else could we do? We couldn't just lay down and die, although some did. We couldn't let ourselves be captured since we would almost certainly be shot. And so, we kept on. Plodding, putting one foot in front of the other, weary beyond belief, pushing ourselves beyond the very boundaries of human endurance.

We were now leaving the Desierto de Calanda and passing through the Sierra del Vizcuerno. The hills weren't quite so high now, and there were stunted trees, tortured and twisted by the cierzo into shapes that defied creation. We weaved our way between rocky outcrops, sometimes clambering over low stone walls left over from farmsteads that had vanished long ago. A few times we reached the top of a rise to find the sheer drop of a cliff face and had to retrace our steps back down the hill and then around rather than over. That was the worst kind of torture, having made a superhuman effort to climb a slope only to have to turn around and retrace our steps. The terrain was littered with huge grey boulders as big as houses and the distant hills rose grey and forbidding before us, seemingly blocking our path.

We were gasping for liquid. Anything. I imagined myself drowning in a huge barrel of the foulest local wine and not wanting to be saved. And as the morning wore on, I pictured myself at the north pole being consumed bit by bit by a slow-moving glacier over the course of several million years. Perhaps I was suffering from heatstroke or dehydration, maybe both at once. Off in the distance, the usual heat-haze mirage that always formed on the upper slopes of the next hill, had become an Icelandic waterfall, tumbling so loud that I could almost hear it. There were times when I had to stop myself from running towards it and diving in headfirst. I craved the relief of an unexpected London shower. One of those cold ones that freezes your brain despite your hat. I think, had I been in

London, I would have leapt into the Thames and drunk it dry.

All throughout the rest of my life, whenever I have felt thirsty, the feeling has always rushed me back to those endless, moisture-less days tramping across the Aragon. Sometimes, I let my thirst develop, I nurture it to see if it could possibly get anywhere near as intense as back them, but that is just impossible to achieve. And the hunger? I often think that had we reached Caspe and found it in the hands of the Rebels like the other towns before it, then we would have surrendered on mass for half a glass of water and a mouthful of cold chickpeas each.

CHAPTER TEN

The route towards Caspe took us through gaps in the hills that slithered like long thin snakes. We passed yet more abandoned farms and tiny olive groves hidden away between huge orange boulders. The old farmhouses showed their naked wooden beams where the roofs had been blown away, and sometimes just a single defiant stone wall remained standing. This whole region had been affected by the war that had divided the Aragon right down the middle, and it was the local people who had paid the price for being on the front line. And now the front line was moving ever further into Republican Aragon, the Rebels pushing through towards the Mediterranean as did the mighty River Ebro. Soon there would be no Republican Aragon. Our only hope was to somehow stem this tide of defeat.

All throughout that morning, as we neared Caspe, we could make out the sound of fighting. Distant like summer thunder to begin with, but gradually increasing in volume. When the town came into sight through a break in the hills, we could see palls of smoke hanging over the high ground to the western side. It looked like we would arrive just in time to take part in the battle. Maybe we could make a difference.

We picked up the pace. What had been a slow and weary grind for the last several days was now a much quicker march. We certainly did not want to arrive too late. It was just such a relief to find Caspe still holding out. Maybe this could be the place that made the definitive stand to stem the Rebel advance. Caspe was the capital of Republican Aragon since Zaragoza, Huesca and Teruel had all declared in favour of the Uprising in its earliest days. It would be, it had to be, defended at all costs. To lose Caspe would be to lose the whole of the rest of the Aragon.

At last, we were over the final hill and walking down into the town. We were easily recognisable as the defeated of previous battles and passed without any problem through the different defensive positions that were covering this route into Caspe. We saw a couple of machinegun posts, but the battle had obviously started away to the west with our troops defending the hills covering the main road from Alcañiz. We had been forced to march across country as the Nationalists had control of the skies. We would have been easy pickings just sticking to that road.

*

Once we reached the town, our priority was water. We found a fountain in the main square and fought for a little space around it in order to get a first mouthful. Those who had drunk that first exquisite drop were quickly dragged aside by those who had not.

We remained in the square for a while, sitting in the shade of a tall building, waiting to be told what to do. In the end, we were fed and allowed to wash before being told to re-join our different units. Walt, Jack and I, along with the other handful of Britishers were pointed in the direction of the railway station where the Battalion was positioned.

We found the headquarters in a two-storey red brick house not far from the station.

"Where 'ave you boys bin?" asked someone with a laugh as we pushed our way into the house.

"Got lost on the way from Belchite," said Walt.

"Well, you're 'ere now. An' just in time," came the Captain's voice. "Go upstairs and get some rest, we'll call you in a few hours."

I wasn't sure I could rest with the sound of artillery fire not too far away and my nerves on edge, but we soon settled down on the wooden floor and I for one was glad to get some sleep.

In the late afternoon, we were sent up ahead, over the railway bridge to reinforce the XIV Brigade who were holding the crossroads where the road out of Caspe divided. The left fork heading for Alcañiz and the right towards Escatrón. Not too far away, the great River Ebro snaked, fat and lazy, as it oozed ever on towards the sea. The bridges were being blown to stop the

Rebels pouring across and deep into Republican territory. This was the last stand before Catalunya.

All through the afternoon, we could hear the incessant sound of an artillery battle. Our guns were firing from the hills that flanked the road to Alcañiz, and the Fascists were firing back at them. Planes circled lazily overhead, watching, and then suddenly diving to release their bombs. Time after time they swooped down, until another hilltop fell silent and the Rebels moved just a little bit closer to the town. They were anxious hours. We knew the inevitable battle was coming. The result seemed inevitable too. I hadn't been a soldier for very long, and I had no experience of anything at all in life, but our army was clearly on the backfoot. There were even murmurings at nightfall as we settled down to sleep, about how the end of the war could be just weeks or even days away. The old hands, who had been through so much, wondered if their luck would hold out just a little longer. They prayed that they might be able to return home in one piece.

For the likes of Jack and myself, and the other newly-arrived Brigadistas, our Spanish war might be a very short one. Of course, it might be shorter still, if just around the corner there was a bullet with our name on. I tried not to think about the possibility of death. Worse still, of course, was the thought of a serious injury. The loss of an arm or a leg. The almost-killer bullet that ripped off the side of your face and left you a monster for the rest of your life. Better to die I thought.

I'd seen death aplenty by now. Far more than a young man of my age back then should ever have seen. I'd seen men ripped apart and scattered in pieces by a bomb dropped from an enemy plane or torn right in two lengthwise by an exploding artillery shell. And then of course the agonising, bullet-ridden death of a machinegun burst. Or, just the solitary death of a single rifle shot to the head. That was the best way to go I concluded, a sniper's hit to the head. You probably wouldn't even know it had happened. Alive one second and nothing at all the next. That would be my chosen death.

There were those who longed for a wound just to get themselves away from the front line, even for a few weeks. A rest in some distant hospital. Anything to be away from the continuing pounding of the heavy guns and the overwhelming stench of fear that every one of us had on our breath. Just a light wound, just one that would give you a ticket to somewhere else and an interesting story to tell for the rest of your life on boring-pub winter evenings. Nobody mentioned self-inflicted wounds, nobody talked about that sort of thing.

Perhaps worse than just death, was the possibility of falling into enemy hands. The Fascists hated all Reds, but foreign Reds were top of their list for revenge. They loathed all those who had come from outside the country in defence of the legitimate government, whilst turning a blind eye to the Italians and Germans who fought for them. And then there was the fear of falling into the hands of Franco's Moroccan troops, the Foreign Legion or Army of Africa. They were rumoured to be looking for revenge against anyone from the International Brigades who had stalled their attack on Madrid just when victory, and probably the end of the war, was in their grasp.

At dusk, we were relieved and sent back across the railway bridge with the promise of food. The good thing about Caspe was that the Brigade had its headquarters there, and there were people doing their best to keep the troops fed and supplied with ammunition.

We were given a ladle of meat stew each, although I for one didn't find any meat in my dish. But the oil that floated on the top did have a slightly meaty taste, so maybe there had been some sort of meat involved in its creation process. I wouldn't have liked to know exactly what type of meat though. There were chunks of potato too, it was a long time since our food had contained potatoes. Then of course there were the ever-present, thick-skinned white beans so typical of that part of Spain. They at least gave you something to chew on and you could certainly feel their presence in your stomach for a time afterwards. We were even given a small loaf of bread each and we drank our fill of water from the fountain.

We sat in the little square at the end of the Avenida de la República and chatted a bit. The guns had fallen silent. For a while, laughter and cigarette smoke filled the air. It was almost possible to forget that in all probability the next day at dawn the enemy would hit us with everything they had. I wondered how many of those sitting there in that square, in the shifting moonlight, would live to see the next nightfall.

Behind us were the wide stone steps leading up to the church with its big arched entrance. It was no longer a place of worship but had been converted into a warehouse to store everything that fighting men could need. Soldiers came and went, in and out of the great wooden doors in far greater numbers than any congregation ever had. Further up the slope but hidden from view was the castle.

We returned to the battalion's red building and found a space up on the top floor to crash out. Walt said that he hoped we would be getting a replacement machinegun the next day, he had been making enquiries. I hoped to god that we wouldn't. I preferred to be a nobody rather than have the responsibility of keeping Walt's machinegun fed with ammunition which was growing scarcer by the day.

We were awoken well before dawn and given a small piece of bread each. Surprisingly it was still warm, which meant that those in charge were still making sure that we were fed and that they hadn't yet abandoned the town, which was a good sign.

Someone had come up with the bright idea that we should make a counterattack at dawn. The enemy thought they had us pinned down and that they had knocked all the fight out of us, the last thing that they would be expecting would be for us to attack them.

We moved quietly forward across the railway bridge and along the road beyond. We paused at the sandbagged position where we had been posted the day before and waited for the command to attack. No command came. Dawn came and still we waited.

Around eleven, we were shepherded up into the hills to try to prevent the fall of yet more high ground. We immediately came under bombardment from the Rebel artillery, and although we tried to dig ourselves somewhere to hide, it wasn't easy. In the end, we were forced to withdraw, another hilltop fell to the enemy. We left behind ten of our number dead and carried back several more wounded comrades. When we reached the main road, we found that our position there had been bombed by planes and was now abandoned. Dead bodies filled the bomb craters and sand filled the air. The way into Caspe was now wide open. We re-crossed the railway bridge and returned to the red house to await further instructions. You could see the worry on the men's faces. It looked for all the world that in no time at all we would be run out of Caspe, just as we had been at Belchite. It also looked like once more we would be the last to leave, expected to hold back the Fascists long enough to allow the rest of our army to scuttle away with their tails between their legs.

All the while, the enemy barrage crept nearer. By mid-afternoon, it was deafening. We knew that at any moment our headquarters might come within range. We were sent out, back over the railway bridge and given orders to hold it at all costs. There was some debate as to whether we should blow the bridge to hold up the Fascist advance for a while, but no orders to do so had been received.

We waited anxiously at the far end of the bridge, peering into the ever-thickening squall of smoke and dust for a first glimpse of the enemy. When they finally came, we were horrified to make out the dreaded Army of Africa. They hadn't expected to meet any real resistance, imaging that this town would be quickly abandoned as had those they had been through before. We let them advance until they saw us and then we opened fire before they could find cover. I fired a couple of shots, glad to realise that my hands were no longer trembling as they had been before, and then the order to cease fire came. We couldn't go wasting bullets shooting at shadows that flitted like ghosts in and out of the spiralling dust.

We could no longer see the Rebel soldiers as their artillery was targeting the bridge and a huge plume of smoke had engulfed them like a thick fog. If the bridge took a direct hit, then we would be cut off. The decision was made to withdraw. Fuck the bridge. We scampered across the rough ground from our position and started to cross the railway bridge. Bullets whistled all around and a huge explosion landed just behind us, almost on top of the position we had so recently vacated. My heart was pounding fit to burst. I reached the bridge and set off across it, I didn't look back, I was aware of others running alongside me or a little in front of me, although I couldn't tell who they were. A bullet struck a metal post just beside me and I was suddenly very aware that at any moment I might be hit.

I tripped and fell as my foot caught on something and I landed with a thump on top of a headless corpse. It scared the life out of me and gave me the sudden surge of adrenalin I needed to get myself back to the other side of the bridge. We found the red house abandoned with its roof blown in.

CHAPTER ELEVEN

The battle for Caspe raged on into the afternoon. We fought a retreat through the narrow streets towards the upper town, falling ever back, towards the square with the church. The castle behind the church, perched on top of the hill, seemed to be our only possible destination.

Any wounded who couldn't manage to keep up were left at the mercy of the enemy. We were desperate to keep ahead of the Fascists, who seemed to be just one corner behind us the whole time. In a little street, not far from the Plaza del Compromiso, we paused to get our breath back. It had been an uphill struggle from the valley, where the railway station was, into the heart of the town, and we were short of breath. I bent double, my hands on my hips, drawing air into my lungs in quick panting gasps. I could feel my heart pounding in my chest, as much from fear as from anything.

Just then a group of fascists rounded the corner. There was nowhere for us to take shelter, the doorways of the houses had all been boarded up when their occupants had sensibly left before the arrival of the enemy. I dropped instantly to my knees, surprising even myself as to how quickly I snatched my rifle off my shoulder and brought it to bear on one of the men who had rushed into the tiny street. He just stood there gaping, like a rabbit caught in a lorry's headlights on a country road. I fired. He fell. I fired again.

I instantly heard more rifles just behind me and realised that others had opened fire too. I was glad that they hadn't panicked and run away to leave me to deal with the enemy alone. Luckily, it was just a small group of men and we were able to overcome them before they got over their initial surprise at finding us there. Just as quickly as it had started, so it was over. One of them had managed to escape back around the corner from where they had appeared, and so without further ado, we pressed on up the sloping street.

We didn't stop again until we reached the square. We had expected to find our own troops massed there to make a stand, but it was deserted. Caspe, just like the other towns and villages of the Aragon before it, had been abandoned. And just as at Belchite, we would be the last to leave. We had been left behind once more. Maybe we had been forgotten in the chaos, but more than likely no one cared enough about us to want to help.

"What now Walt?" I asked.

"I'd say we's well and truly fucked," said the big man.

There was nowhere left for us to go except further upwards. We raced across the square and up the steps that ran beside the cathedral. We hadn't got halfway before I heard the first shot fired at us. A bullet whizzed by close to my left ear and thudded into the stone wall of the cathedral. I didn't look back to see how many Rebels had already reached the square, I just kept running. The flight of steps was steep and seemed to take forever. At last we reached the top. We paused for breath and fired off a shot or two from the shelter of the wall. We didn't expect to hit anyone, just to make it clear that we were still going to fight rather than surrender. The thought of surrender at that moment filled me with far greater dread than the thought of death. I think everyone felt the same, otherwise why would we have kept running?

We reached the castle. The gate was open wide. Everyone was gone. A quick inspection of the courtyard showed the way the place had been abandoned in some haste. A black car with the driver's door open and the keys in the ignition drew our attention and one of the men ran over and tried to start it up. The engine just spluttered like a choking death and refused to start. The driver had obviously run out of petrol or the petrol had been removed and used for some more important vehicle.

There were discarded bits of uniform, empty boxes that had once contained something useful like grenades or ammunition, and pieces of paper everywhere. Maybe someone had thought to bring out the files into the courtyard to burn every piece of paperwork they could lay their hands on. But they had run out of time and just dropped everything and fled.

We didn't hang about, there was nothing for us there except capture. We exited through the same gate and a shot rang out. I heard a muffled scream behind me but didn't turn to look. We ran as fast as we could around to the back of the castle. The cliff face was sheer, and we seemed to be trapped. What should we do? We could head back around to the front of the castle and face certain death at the hands of the Rebels, or we could throw ourselves off the cliff and die in the ravine below.

One of the men had walked a little way ahead of the rest of us, along the top of the cliff. He seemed to be peering down the cliff face. He turned and ran back over to us.

"I think there's a way down," he said. "Follow me."

We didn't need to be told twice. We charged after him, condemned men given an unexpected last-minute reprieve. We all stopped when we reached the place where he had been. Looking down I don't think any of us could see what he had supposedly seen, but when he disappeared over the ledge dropping out of view, we just followed him like lemmings. And just in time too. From the castle, we could hear excited random gunfire that signified that the Rebels had decided that the town was now theirs and no further resistance was expected.

We stumbled and fell, picked ourselves up and tripped again and again. Sometimes I grabbed at a clump of tough grass to steady myself rather than fall off the side. Fortunately, the Rebel army didn't expect anyone to have found a long-forgotten goat track leading down from the castle. I decided to just look at my feet as we squeezed along the sheer edge of the cliff face, sometimes climbing slightly, always following the lines of the contours of the rocks, before dipping steeply down again. And we scrambled and fell and cursed and sweated and worked our way slowly down, ever downwards, towards the valley floor below and some sort of imagined salvation.

It took us maybe a couple of hours, I don't really know. The stress from the panic of the battle, the sheer terror of it all, was slowly sinking in. My body was entering into a state of fatigue and I felt my legs trembling. I was worried that they might just give way and buckle underneath me. If they did, then I would fall crashing down the cliffside to the valley below. The lack of food and water was making me dizzy, but there was no time to stop for a drink or anything. All that mattered was getting away from the enemy. Their presence in the castle above us was always there. The sound of motor vehicles and the rapid fire of a volley of shots that probably meant that executions were already taking place. We'd heard stories of the Rebels entering a town and rounding up anyone they could find and just shooting them. They certainly didn't want to make the mistake of leaving a single Red alive.

We paused briefly at the bottom of the cliff face and took a quick drink of water from our bottles. Then we were ready to put as much distance between ourselves and Caspe as possible come nightfall.

Ahead of us, through the Sierra de Caspe, somewhere miles away, was the last hope of safety, Catalunya. The land was once more rolling hills, dotted with skeletal orchards and dwarf olive groves, signs of a life that had existed unchanged for generations, but which was now gone for good. I don't think anyone at that time could imagine that there could ever again be peace, or that life could return to how it had always been.

We set off in determined fashion, watching the ground at our feet so as not to trip over the shattered rocks that littered the path. We skirted between huge black boulders, some of which had been split open by centuries of freezing winters and fiery summers to reveal a startling orange interior. We were glad to be away from Caspe of course, but once again we were fleeing across country in desperate search of somewhere that was still in Loyalist hands.

The Rebels had pushed through the Republican half of the Aragon in quick time. What was to stop them just continuing into Catalunya and sweeping all before them until they reached the Pyrenees? It was obvious to everyone that the situation was desperate. The Republic was on the verge of collapse, but no one mentioned defeat. We were soldiers and this was our war. We would keep on fighting until told to no longer do so, or until the bullet with our name on finally caught up with us. Maybe up on some desolate hillside in the middle of nowhere, or in the narrow backstreets of some tiny nameless village.

As it began to grow dark, looking backwards, we could just make out the last glowing fires still to be extinguished in Caspe. We began to search for somewhere to shelter for the night. Up ahead, we saw a small pine forest and we were instinctively drawn towards it. As we approached, we made out an old abandoned farmhouse that had been built into the side of a cliff face. Its roof had collapsed in, long ago, but its walls might well provide some protection from the cold as the night came and the cierzo began to wander through the hills in search of victims.

Suddenly, a shot rang out. It came from the direction of the farmhouse and the pine forest. Almost as one we instantly dropped to the ground, trying desperately to mould ourselves into the ragged surface of the track we had been walking along. We were relatively exposed. Once on our bellies we would have to try to crawl to a boulder or something for cover. Another shot came.

I remember feeling a jagged rock digging into my chest and cutting me through my thin shirt, but I didn't want to raise myself even slightly in order to remove it. Every time someone moved, another shot rang out. I kept totally still, frozen, moulded into the very ground beneath me. Someone had managed to reach some cover and began to return fire. This forced our opponents to keep their heads down and allowed more of our number to crawl to the relative safety of a nearby boulder. Still out in the open, I became the main target for those who were shooting at us, even though now their firing was hurried and less frequent as my comrades tried to keep them pinned down.

"Jesus," muttered Walt, snarling in my direction, "get the fuck out of there will ya."

I don't know exactly why, it was a stupid thing to do, but suddenly I leapt to my feet and rushed across to the nearest boulder. Bullets followed me like angry wasps, stinging the ground around my feet or snapping at the air just in front of my face. I dived the last few feet and landed in a cloud of dust.

Someone shouted out "Fascist bastards," at us in Spanish. It was one of the few phrases we recognised. It was then we realised that we were being fired on by our own side.

"Amigos," shouted out Walt. "Compañeros."

The firing stopped. We lay panting behind our boulders and waited for a reply. When it came, we didn't understand what was being said since none of our group spoke any real Spanish. Walt had been in Spain the longest and so we looked at him and waited to see what he would do.

"Fuck it," he cursed under his breath. "Ingleses," he shouted out as loudly as he could "internacionales." And then, slowly, very slowly, he raised himself up from behind the rock where he had been lying. Eventually, he reached his full height and held his rifle out to the side to show he had no intention of firing it. I held my breath. If they took Walt down, I didn't know what I would do. I relied on him to get me through from hour to hour.

"Comrades!" came the response, and with that I saw Walt breathe a sigh of relief and head slowly away from us towards the farmhouse. One by one, the rest of us got wearily to our feet and followed him. I kept myself doubled over as much as possible in case the shooting began again, but soon we saw someone emerge from the farmhouse door and start walking towards Walt.

The two men paused briefly and then shook hands. That was the signal that everything was all right, and other men began to emerge from the farmhouse door and from amidst the pine trees.

There were far more of them than us, so had the fire fight continued, we would surely all have been killed. Fortunately, neither them nor us had managed to kill anyone and no harm had been done. We congratulated ourselves on being terrible shots.

Jack and I found a spot at the base of a dwarf pine and leaned back against its gnarled trunk and closed our eyes to rest for a while. I could hear stumbling attempts at conversation, possibly about what had happened at Caspe or where we should go next, but I didn't care, and I guess I fell asleep.

I was awoken after a few hours by Walt and told to keep watch for a while. It was dark. Jack was to keep me company. We crawled to the edge of the trees and lay on our stomachs with our rifles close at hand. There were the usual sounds of the night, a tortured owl or a flurry of bats, the cierzo rustling the pine needles above our heads. And then the sounds of men at rest, a cough, a curse, a thunderous snore. That would be Walt I guessed.

Occasionally, I would whisper something to Jack, but he never once replied. His regular deep breathing told me that he was asleep, but I was glad he was there, and I continued to whisper to him all throughout that long night. I told him how glad I was to have him there with me, how I would never have survived so long without him, and that I hoped that somehow we might make it back to England together and go back to the lives we had known before. I didn't like being a soldier, and I was tired of being scared all the time. The hunger and exhaustion I could handle, it was the fear I hated.

If we were supposed to have been relieved at some stage during the night, it never happened, and so we remained there on the edge of the pine forest, on a soft bed of fallen needles, until the sky began to lighten. The war was set to continue for another day, and I wondered if jack and I would be lucky enough to still be alive come its end.

CHAPTER TWELVE

Walt apologised for not sending us someone to take over the watch during the night. He said that he thought the Spanish would send someone, but I think he just fell into a deep sleep and never woke until dawn. I could understand, he must have been mentally and physically exhausted, not just from what we had already been through, but also from having to worry about what was to come. At least we had found some fellow stragglers and difficult decisions could be shared.

The Spanish unit that we had stumbled across at the end of the previous afternoon had been one of the last to leave Caspe and had managed to grab some small loaves of bread from an abandoned bakery before leaving. These they generously shared with us, seeing as we had nothing. Someone had made a fire, and some water was being boiled with a handful of green pine needles in it as some sort of tea. Jack and I shared a small cup, and at least it was something warm to start the day.

We didn't hang around long. After a night's rest in Caspe, the Rebels would be thinking about continuing their advance and their push for victory. It occurred to me that the war could be over in a matter of weeks, maybe even days. What would happen to us then?

Would we be taken care of, or would we be abandoned to the mercy of Franco. We might be herded into a bullring somewhere and machinegunned. I had heard someone say that something like that had already happened at some place called Badajoz, but maybe it was just exaggerated war gossip.

Leaving the relative safety of the pine forest, we were once again in open country. The low hills had sharp pointed tops. We stumbled between them on pathways made by goats and not really fit for soldiers, most of whom didn't have adequate footwear. The Spanish soldiers nearly all wore rope-soled shoes and it must have been hell for them. At least Jack and I had our boots, but they were fast wearing out. Some of the other Brigadistas also had boots, probably taken from a dead Fascist since their equipment seemed to be far superior in quality to our own. We didn't look like you might imagine soldiers to look, we were not dressed up for parade with shiny buttons trimmed beards and slicked-back hair. This was real soldiering, uniforms almost rigid like cardboard after days on end of sweat and dust, a random array of headgear that would have been left untouched at a jumble sale, rope for the soles of shoes and string keeping up trousers that in some cases had more holes than cloth.

We had no real sense of where to go, the priority was still to distance ourselves from Caspe as fast as we could. We were vaguely heading in the direction of Catalunya. I for one would be glad to see the back of the Aragon, in fact I hoped never to see it again for the rest of my life. For me it had been a living hell and I was sure I would always remember it so.

Around mid-morning, we reached a once-grand farmhouse surrounded by orchards of low trees, possibly peach trees someone said, but they had been neglected and left to dry out and only a handful had any leaves on them. There were also a few dwarf olive trees, which seemed to have better resisted the years of neglect and lack of irrigation. These orchards were enclosed by low stone walls and made it clear that this had once been an important property, but it seemed to have been abandoned long before the war.

Here we found a larger group of our own forces who had spent the night sheltering in the house or amongst the trees within the safety of the old stone walls. They were preparing to move on. Men were smoking a shared cigarette or tidying up their bed rolls, someone was shaving, although personally I wouldn't have wasted my meagre water ration on that.

The Spaniard who seemed to have taken charge of our little group, took Walt with him into the house to find out what was going on. The rest of us sat down on a wall and waited.

They emerged with a short balding captain who looked old enough to be my grandfather. Walt was carrying a scrap of paper in his hand. The Captain shouted at his men and we watched them get into a group and then start to move out. We got to our feet to follow them. Walt held his hand up to Jack and I to indicate that we should stay put.

The rest of our group listened to some brief explanation of what was going on, and I understood the name Batea which was spoken several times and was therefore I presumed our destination. The others rose to their feet and wearily began to follow the Captain's little column.

Jack and I remained with Walt, wondering just what the hell was going on.

"Well boys," he began, mumbling and avoiding eye contact with us which was strange in itself, "we've been given a special little mission."

"What's up, Walt?" asked Jack.

"There's a fuel dump somewhere near here and we need to blow it up before the enemy get there."

"Why us?" I wanted to know.

"Don't be a stupid fuck," snapped Walt. It was obvious why us.

"Oh shit!" exclaimed Jack.

"Oh shit exactly," agreed Walt. He pulled a hunk of stale bread from his pocket and broke it into three roughly equal pieces and shared it with us. He had probably been told to choose who was to go with him, and of course, he had chosen his two little shadows. His lack of eye contact and the sharing of his last piece of bread indicated that he was feeling guilty. He needn't have felt bad. I for one would have followed him down to the depths of hell. I was pretty sure that Jack felt the same. Maybe that was where we were going anyway.

We stalked off in the direction of the supposed fuel dump. I wasn't convinced that we would find anything at all, it seemed unlikely to me that our army would have a fuel supply it hadn't already used in the rush to flee from the Aragon.

So, we were on our own. Three isolated foreigners walking around in no man's land. Just as likely to be shot by our own side as by the enemy.

We cut straight across open country. There were no goat tracks anymore, not in the direction we were going. We spread out, Walt in the middle and jack and I on either side. Our eyes were straining, scanning the horizon for some sign of life and our ears were on full alert for the sound of planes. All around was scrubland, knee-high dry grass littered with rocks that tried repeatedly to trip us. In the distance, the two low hills between which we had to pass, pointed like praying hands up towards an uncaring god.

The wind tugged at our ragged clothes and blew dust into our eyes trying to push us back to where we had started from. We trudged on regardless. We were determined to get the job done as quickly as possible and then head for Batea and Catalunya. We had to hope, as the whole Republic had to hope, that the Rebels would not push on through into Catalunya but would content themselves with the capture of the Aragon. If they paused to regroup and to think about what to do next, it gave our troops the chance to recover from this wave of continuous defeat. Maybe the Republic could still get over this latest setback, hadn't Madrid held out when all hope seemed lost? Perhaps the much talked-about European war would start, and non-intervention would end and the fight in Spain might become part of a broader picture.

It dawned on me that there was a very high possibility that we might be captured out here on our own. A motorised column could suddenly come out of nowhere, and there was certainly nowhere to hide and nowhere to run to.

We didn't talk to each other that long morning. We simply made laborious progress across the uneven ground, just pausing on a couple of occasions to drink a quick mouthful of water and for Walt and Jack to smoke a shared cigarette. The sun was high in the sky and a prickly sweat raged across my back beneath my sticky shirt. There was no shelter, not a single tree and rarely even a small bush. It was a desolate plain and the sooner we could cross it the better.

All the while, in the distance, the two hills between which we had to pass, seemed to be advancing at an even greater pace than we were. I tried not to look ahead for a while with the hope that when I did so again, I might find the hills almost within touching distance. I looked away to my left, looking for something to take my eyes and my mind off the direction we were going. There was nothing, no trees, no isolated farm buildings, not even the typical low stone walls we were used to seeing everywhere. It was like we were the first people ever to walk there.

Gradually, as if we were walking through quicksand, the hills began to rise into view at last, climbing slowly up to their full height. We clambered up the slope of the nearest one to find a bit of shelter from the sun under the lip of a huge boulder. We took a sip of water and let our eyes take a break from the sun's nagging glare. We were tired, but we knew we couldn't rest for long. Walt studied his little hand-drawn map, hoping I think that it would not only tell him where to go, but also what to do when we got there. He had been given a couple of grenades in order to accomplish our mission, but there was always the possibility that they were duds. It happened a lot.

It was already mid-afternoon, and we couldn't delay much longer. Walt's map showed a cluster of buildings by a road somewhere beyond the two hills. Just beyond them the fuel dump was marked with a jagged X.

We scrambled down the slope amid a flurry of scree and took up walking once more. It was a hot afternoon, and I could feel the sun on my neck and the sweat prickling my eyes. According to the map, we didn't have far to go, but who knew if the map was to any sort of scale and which madman had been responsible for drawing it.

After an hour or so, we saw some low houses huddled together ahead of us, down in a valley. They were made of clay bricks the same colour as the landscape and their roofs were tiled and although they were obviously poor dwellings they didn't seem to have been abandoned. We immediately levelled our rifles pointing in front of us and hurried towards them. At that precise moment, there was no sign of life, maybe the people who had lived there had fled, maybe they were sheltering indoors from the heat. But we couldn't take any chances.

As we came up to the first of the houses, Walt told Jack and I to lie flat and be ready to provide covering fire. He said that he was going to check the buildings one by one. We lay flat on the hard, stony ground and watched the big man slowly approach the first house. I realised that my heart was thumping wildly, so loud that I could hear it inside my head. It was possible that Walt was just about to barge in on a group of resting Fascists and all hell was going to break loose.

I had my rifle trained on the door of the nearest dwelling and Jack had his sights set on a side window. There was an eerie silence hanging over the place. We held our breath as Walt put his ear against the faded blue wooden door to work out if there might be anyone inside.

CHAPTER THIRTEEN

Walt kept his ear glued to the door for several minutes. He then tried to open it. It was locked. He moved onto the next house. Jack and I changed our position to offer him cover if needed. For each new dwelling it was the same routine: listening, trying the door and then moving on. After the last house he beckoned us to him.

"There's no one 'ere," he mumbled, "let's keep goin'."

We walked away from the little abandoned cluster of houses, straight ahead as the map indicated. I hoped it wouldn't be much farther. Just the three of us alone, we couldn't hope to take on a Fascist patrol. The sooner we got this over with the better.

We pressed on further down into the valley. In the distance, we could see neat fields covered in ordered vines, but no one was working there now. They must belong to the people from the abandoned houses we had just come from. Beyond the vineyards was a small hill and clinging to the top a stone church. Walt didn't say anything, but instinctively we headed towards it. It was a strange place for a church, stuck on a hill in the middle of nowhere.

As we approached, we saw that it was a poor man's place of worship, squat with a dwarf tower topped by a wooden cross that was leaning slightly to one side. Maybe it was the site of some long-forgotten miracle.

We climbed up the side of the hill on a path that was overgrown and hadn't been used for years. Finally, we reached the church. The door was broken in and inside the place was black from fire. The wooden pews had burnt away almost entirely and the large round window at the far end had no glass. Some startled pigeons began to circle around above our heads.

We left the church and instead walked around the top of the hill peering off into the distance. We had a good view. But there was nothing to see. The only thing of any note were the neat vineyards and the cluster of single-storey houses, we had already passed through. On all other sides, there was nothing out of the ordinary.

Walt walked three times around the church on the top of the hill, looking forlornly out over the desolate landscape on every side. He desperately wanted to see a fuel dump that we could blow up, but he had to conclude that it was either gone or that, more than likely, it had never existed in the first place. Someone might have wanted a fuel dump there. It might have been plotted on some General's campaign map, but the fuel had never arrived. In the failing Republic, fuel was liquid gold.

"What should we do now?" I asked Walt.

"We should get the hell out of 'ere," he replied.

"Where Walt?" asked Jack.

"Back to that farm, and then to Batea. Weren't that where they said?"

"It were," agreed Jack. I nodded.

"Let's fuckin' get a move on then," decided Walt.

We left the church, scrambling down the hillside and back the way we had come, climbing slowly up out of the valley. It was late afternoon, I worried that we might not make it back to the farm before nightfall. I really didn't want to be stuck out in the open in the middle of nowhere.

When we reached the little group of abandoned houses past the vineyards, we skirted around them. I asked if it might be a good idea to spend the night there, but Walt disagreed. We had to get back to the farm, get a few hours rest and then try to catch up with the remainder of our group the next day. If we didn't, it was bad news, he didn't have a fucking clue where Batea was, he said. It wasn't even marked on his useless map. In fact, he had screwed it up into a ball and thrown it over the hillside from up by the church.

We passed through the gap in the two, pointed hills without stopping and headed back across the barren scrubland in the direction of the farm. By nightfall, we had only made it about halfway, but after a quick drink of water we hurried on. There was a pale half-moon, hanging above the distant mountains and it served to illuminate our way. There was a black smudge directly ahead that we knew to be the pine forest where the farm was.

We had walked at night before. We had walked at night tired and hungry. We just trudged on, heads bowed and tried not to think of anything except putting one foot in front of the other. It was a routine we knew all too well. Occasionally, one of us would trip over a white rock hidden amongst the white grass and sprawl to the ground. The only thing to do was to pick yourself up, dust yourself down and get going again. We carried our rifles slung over our shoulders rather than at the ready. We didn't think the enemy would be patrolling in the hours of darkness. They would be resting in one of the villages they had captured, eat captured food which would taste twice as sweet, and sleep in captured beds. Then, the next morning, they would awake refreshed and ready to push on into Catalunya. Victory was within their grasp.

It occurred to me, that we might be the only three Loyalist soldiers left alive or uncaptured in the Aragon. We had been the last to leave Belchite, the last to leave Caspe and it was fitting that we should be the last to leave the Aragon. It was possible that the retreat would just continue through into Catalunya, town by town, village by village, until we were trapped against the French border. Would the French government open the border to let us escape? Or would they keep it closed and allow the Rebels to carry out one final grand massacre?

The wind began to pick up, tugging at our shirts, pushing us sideways and then backwards as it seemed to change direction constantly, any direction other than forward. The cierzo had arrived, a demon in the darkness. We struggled onwards our faces whipped by flying earth.

At last, we began to make out the shapes of the trees of the little pine forest not too far off. As we got nearer, so the farmhouse began to emerge from the darkness. Its stonewalls reflected the moonlight as did the trunks of the trees so that everything was a ghostly white. I breathed a sigh of relief. We had been walking all day and into the night, but at last we could have a rest. We were sweating from our constant walking, but we knew that the night around us was cold, and it would be good to be inside the farmhouse and protected from the gathering cierzo by its sturdy walls.

Jack and I sat on a low wall whilst Walt went to check out the house. I don't know why we did that. He didn't tell us to. Maybe he didn't have to anymore, we had come so far together. I took my rifle off my shoulder and laid it on the top of the wall, then I removed my pack and began to pull out my blanket. Jack was bent down untying his boots.

Suddenly, we heard a shout of alarm from the direction of the farmhouse. Walt was standing with the door open, desperately trying to free a grenade from his belt. There was an answering scream from whoever was inside. Jack and I instantly dropped to our knees and fumbled for our rifles, I grabbed mine from on top of the wall and quickly brought it to bear pointing in the direction of the house. Walt had released his grenade and pulled the pin. A shot rang out, then a second. I saw Walt stagger from the double impact in his chest and then he disappeared into the house.

A second or two later, there was a huge explosion. We saw its fiery strength through the little side window, through the holes in the roof and back out through the door. The whole house seemed to shudder from the blast and rise out of the ground before falling back into place, whole rather than in pieces. Jack grabbed my arm.

"Run Billy," he shouted.

"We can't leave Walt," I shouted back.

"Walt's dead you idiot." And he tugged me by the arm so hard that it hurt, and the pain made me act. We jumped over the wall and set off into the pine forest. I don't know whether Jack took that direction intentionally or not, but it was the right way to head. There was no point in fleeing back towards Caspe.

We were fortunate that there were no Fascists in amongst the trees. It had most likely been a small advanced patrol which had left it too late to return to Caspe for the night. They had stumbled across the little farmhouse and decided to hole up there to shelter from the cierzo, as had been our intention.

We ran and stumbled through the pine trees in a world of darkness. The moon couldn't penetrate the forest, but a distant glow on the far side told us where to head. I remember constantly tripping over fallen branches and crashing to my hands and knees. Jack was always a little ahead of me, always calling out to me, telling me to pick myself up when I fell, urging me onwards and away from danger.

We didn't stop when we reached the edge of the forest, but ran on in a mad panic, until finally we could run no more. We both bent over double, hands on knees and panted like crazed dogs. The night air was cold in our lungs. I realised that I had left my blanket and pack behind in the panic to save our lives. Jack had done the same and one of his boots was still unlaced. All we had were our rifles and the ammunition left in our pouches. We had no food and no water, and no idea which way to head.

We didn't rest long. There was the very real possibility that some of the Fascists might have survived the explosion in the farmhouse or that there was another patrol close by. We didn't need to speak about it, we just straightened up and got going again. I could feel my legs trembling and my heart was racing.

I never told Jack that I hated him for getting me into this war, I didn't think he'd want to hear it. Anyway, it was hard to hate someone when they were the only friend you had in the whole world. He was even more important to me now since Walt was dead. It was hard to believe. He had seemed so strong, invincible almost, but now he was gone. And Jack was all I had, and now I would look to him for leadership as I always had back in London. Did he want the responsibility? I don't know, I didn't ask. It was just how it had always been. And so, I followed just a couple of paces behind him, trusting him to get me to safety.

In the vague moonlight, I could see that we were walking into an area of low hills. The sides had been cut to form terraces, and within low stone walls there were neatly spaced dwarf olive trees.

I felt the first spots of rain on my face, blown in hard by the cierzo. It seemed determined to push us back into the arms of the Fascists. As we trudged on, the wind increased in strength and the rain became heavier. My teeth began to chatter. I began to feel cold and miserable.

"We ought to take shelter Jack," I shouted into the face of the wind.

"An' where d'you think we should do that?" he snapped back.

I scanned the hillsides around us for some sort of lean-too dwelling or even an overhanging cliff we could huddle under. Then on the slope of the next hill, I saw one of those little stone shelters that the shepherds used during bad weather. I had thought them a waste of time, but now it was a godsend. I pointed it out to Jack, and we hurried over to it, climbing rapidly up the hillside just as a storm began.

We reached the little shelter that was sort of shaped like a beehive. By the first flash of lightning we saw that the door was missing, if it ever had one, and that the floor was littered with stones. We quickly scraped away at the floor to create an area just big enough for us both to sit down with our backs against the cold stone walls. It was designed to be just big enough for one man to curl up inside to sleep.

We sat there together, watching the lightning flashes illuminate the brutal landscape through which we had been making our escape and feeling the ground vibrate with every terrific boom of thunder. The rain got heavier as the night wore on, but the thick stone slabs of the shelter's roof kept out the worst of it.

Sometime in the early hours of the morning, the cierzo must have moved the storm onto someplace else, and we must have fallen asleep, uncomfortable though we were. We were exhausted. I don't think I've ever felt so miserable as I did that night, lost up on a hillside on the edge of the Aragon, the wind whistling through the gaps in our stone shelter. Just Jack and I alone and Walt no longer with us.

Come the morning, it was as if there had never been a storm. We emerged from our little shelter and found that life was back to normal. The sun was climbing and there were birds squabbling in the olive groves. We didn't really know which way to go, but we knew we had to go somewhere.

We were following some sort of path without a clue as to where it would take us, but men had been this way before us and that seemed the best that we could hope for. The landscape around us was changing, I thought perhaps we had finally escaped from the Aragon and had entered Catalunya. This area wasn't as desolate and as abandoned as previous zones we had walked across. As well as the walled olive groves up and above us cut into the hillsides, there were little clusters of fruit trees, their branches just starting to bud with new green shoots. Even in the grip of war and destruction, nature still found the strength to carry on.

In the distance, the hills were wrapped in a blanket of lush green pine trees. From time to time, we saw up on the hillsides a lone tree covered in early white blossom. On the floor all around each one there was a white carpet like snow, thrown there by the cierzo and the storm during the previous night.

At midday, with the sun directly above us, we came to a little river running between vineyards and after a good drink of water and a quick wash, we sat down to rest under an ancient fig tree. Jack curled up in the shade and went to sleep, whilst I sat up with my back against the trunk of the tree and watched ants scurrying around in the dirt. It occurred to me that when Jack woke up, we could follow the river in the hope that it would lead us to civilisation. It seemed to be flowing in the right direction.

CHAPTER FOURTEEN

When Jack awoke an hour or so later, I told him my idea about following the river. It was fast-flowing and swollen due to the overnight rain, and the water was red like the earth all around us. He seemed to consider my suggestion for a while, and then with a nod of his head agreed, and we set off walking along the riverbank. Without the river to guide us, we would have continued straight ahead where there was a range of hills topped with clouds smeared with grey. Instead we followed the curve of the river as it bent to the contours of the landscape and took us into a long valley.

We arrived at some vineyards and saw a little stone house. There was smoke coming out of the chimney. We hid behind an isolated olive tree on the edge of the property and watched the house. It was mid-afternoon, and whoever lived there was inside avoiding the hottest part of the day. After a while, Jack decided that we ought to see who was inside. Maybe we could beg some food. The sensible thing to do would be to skirt around this isolated house and continue onwards in the hope of reaching a village before nightfall, but our stomachs were ruling our heads.

Jack told me to stay where I was, whilst he went to investigate, but I said I would go. We had lost Walt. If

I lost Jack, then I was finished. If I was killed, well I guessed Jack would be able to carry on without me.

I took a deep breath, held my rifle out in front of me, and headed towards the house. It was squat, a single storey, a ramshackle roof. I had no grenades like Walt, so my grand plan, should I find Fascists there, was to turn and run away as fast as I could.

The house seemed so small and insignificant, so isolated from the rest of the world, that it was impossible to think that the Rebels might have found it too. Indeed, I had to wonder if the person or people living there had even heard that there had been a military uprising and that the country was in the middle of a civil war. Did they even know which side they were on?

Well, today, whichever side they might or might not be on, the war had finally arrived. I found my heart racing and my whole body was shaking. What had so recently happened to Walt was uppermost in my mind and I was crazy with fear. I tried to take a couple of deep breaths as I approached the door to the property. I didn't know whether to simply barge in and start firing or to knock and to wait for someone to open the door. In the end, I decided on the latter course of action, since it seemed impossible to me that there would be Rebels in this meaningless place.

Holding my rifle in my right hand I knocked on the wooden, glass-less door with my left fist. Then, quickly I stepped back and brought my rifle up to point at the door.

There was no reaction. After several minutes, I knocked again. This time I heard someone coughing and a shuffling of feet, and at long last the ancient door creaked open just a fraction. An old man's face appeared. His face exploded into shock and he tried to shut the door, but I had been expecting that and I stuck my foot in the gap and shoved with all my might. The old man stumbled backwards, and the door flew open.

I walked into the darkened interior, the man now cowering in a corner, my gun pointing at his head. I heard a female scream away to my right and swivelled with my rifle. An old woman had emerged from another room and was understandably shocked to see a soldier in her home.

She began screaming at me in her language but of course I couldn't understand her words, but I knew she was afraid. The old man was mumbling at me, maybe he was begging me not to shoot his wife, I don't know. I turned back towards the door and shouted for Jack. He would know what to do.

When he rushed inside, the old woman began to scream twice as loud, as if a whole army had appeared. Jack made gestures at her that she should calm down, trying to persuade her that we weren't there to do her harm. Eventually, she seemed to get the message and she stopped screaming.

"Brigadistas," Jack informed her. "Republicanos."

This seemed to pacify the woman somewhat. She might have been expecting the whole Fascist army to pass this way, or the dreaded Army of Africa. Instead we were just too frightened foreign boys that had been left behind in the great retreat. In this part of Spain, the population would be anti-Fascist, if not from belief then certainly from circumstance. Whether we were still just in the Aragon or now in Catalunya didn't matter, this area had been in Loyalist hands throughout the war. That of course was now going to change, and that must have been a terrible prospect for ordinary people like this old couple. Republican anti-Fascist propaganda had filled the heads of the civilian population with tales of what the Rebel soldiers would do when they conquered new territories. No wonder the couple were terrified.

"Hambre," said Jack pointing at his mouth. It was one of those essential words that we had soon picked up in Spain. Hambre was the thing that most dominated our thoughts when we weren't under fire from the enemy.

The woman said something to her husband, and he nodded his head. She retreated into the room where she had been before our arrival which was like a small kitchen and larder. There were strings of garlic and onions hanging from the wooden ceiling beams which were just rough tree trunks painted brown. There were also strings of chorizos from the last time someone had butchered a pig. She reached up with a trembling hand and took down a string. She handed it to Jack who was closest to her and then made a sign that we should go. She then began to shout all over again. In the low room her noise was unbearable, and Jack and I retreated outside. We hadn't found any Fascists and we had been given something to eat, so there seemed no point in hanging around any longer and causing the old couple any further distress. Just before she shut the door jack turned back to her.

"Batea?" he asked. The woman paused, looked at us, maybe realising that we were lost and helpless and certainly no threat to her, and she stepped outside. She pointed in the direction that the river was following and then made a sweeping gesture with her hand that seemed to signify that we still had quite some distance to travel. At least we now knew that we were heading in the right direction. Then she closed the door and we heard a deadbolt being drawn across. We took it as our cue to leave them alone.

We walked on a little further and then sat down by the river and ate some of the chorizo. It was tough as old boots, but we weren't complaining. I could have eaten it all then and there, but Jack decided we should keep some for another time, and he gave me a piece which I tucked into my half-empty ammunition pouch. We filled our water bottles with fresh red river water and then set off once more.

I could feel my stomach gurgling and churning, going through the process of breaking down the chorizo that I had just fed it. It was a great feeling to have finally had something to eat, and we both walked along by that nameless river with a renewed energy. It was a huge relief to know that we were heading in the right direction for Batea. We just had to hope that the Fascists wouldn't have taken it before we got there. Experience, of course, told me that it would already have fallen, and then where would we go? It was like being stuck in some repeating daily nightmare. How many villages had we looked to for salvation? I had lost count, and apart from Caspe I had forgotten their names. They all just seemed to blend into one endless disappointment. And what about Batea? Would it just be another name to add to the list and then forget?

I pushed these thoughts to the back of my mind. I certainly didn't say anything to Jack, although more than likely he was worrying about the same things. The afternoon went slowly by, much slower than the flow of the river beside us, but eventually we came to a road. There was an old stone bridge that crossed the river, and the road then wound away to the right into the distance towards some low hills. This was irrigated land with raised channels carrying water from the river to distant fields.

We walked onto the bridge and I looked down at the surging red water whilst Jack studied the scenery around us, trying to decide which way to go. He spent a long time, glancing first one way and then the other along the road. The other option of course was to keep following the river. I think I would have chosen that option myself, it had brought us good luck so far, but what did I know. I kept quiet. I didn't want to be the one to be responsible if we chose the wrong direction and walked straight into the hands of a Fascist patrol.

After a long while, Jack had reached his decision and we crossed the bridge onto the other side of the river and set off along the road. He was right of course in his thinking, roads linked towns and villages in the most direct way possible, whilst the river might meander around for days before getting us somewhere. The river had been fine when it had been our only real option, but now we abandoned it and chose the road.

It was a narrow road, dusty and stony showing little signs of use, but it must lead somewhere. Off to both sides, on the irrigated land were vineyards, neat and tidy and waiting for the spring to arrive in full force. There was an occasional stone lean to, but we didn't see any farmhouses for quite a while, and when we did pass one, it was in ruins up on a hillside.

Towards dusk, the road began to climb up through the hills and our pace began to slow. It had been another long day and I for one was ready to start thinking about somewhere to bed down for the night. I thought the next abandoned farmhouse would be just right. Maybe we might be lucky enough to come across another little shelter like the one we had used during the storm, although that was the last one we had seen. Maybe in Catalunya they didn't build them.

Just as we reached the top of the hill, a shot rang out. I heard Jack scream and saw him collapse to the ground, just falling forward onto the road. A terrible panic gripped me, and I didn't know what to do. I heard another shot and a bullet whizzed past, too close for comfort. I dropped to my knees desperately trying to shrug my rifle off my shoulder and bring it to bear. No sooner had I got it in my hands than I felt a violent blow to my left arm. It was so violent that it punched me around and span me to the floor. I had been hit.

They say that when you're about to die, your whole life flashes before your eyes, but for me it did not. I did seriously think I was about to die though. The only thing I had in my mind was my friend. I had to get to him. I had to somehow get him to safety. I had to do that for him. He had done so much for me. And yet, my motives were entirely selfish, I just couldn't bear the thought of life without him. I just didn't think I could go on alone. A bullet thudded into the ground not far from my head. That decided me. I wasn't just going to lay there in the dust and wait for the bastards to get their aim right. I pushed myself up with my right arm and managed to get up onto my knees. Jack was lying a little further ahead, sprawled face down, a circle of blood around his head. It didn't look good. I had to reach him, I had to save him. I was aware of shouting not far off and the sound of people running towards me, but I blocked out everything and instead thought only of getting across to Jack. It wasn't far, just a few feet. One superhuman effort and I could make it. And yet, I was beginning to feel a nausea creeping up from my stomach and a dizziness invading my brain.

CHAPTER FIFTEEN

From my kneeling position, I lurched forward and threw myself towards Jack. I reached him as quickly as I could and turned my back on the direction that the shots had come from to try to shield him from taking a further hit. I tried to roll him over and managed to half turn him so that I could see his face. I cradled his head in my hands and looked down at him. His face was ghostly white, his eyes half closed. His lips pale.

"Jack, Jack, don't die mate," I begged him.

After a moment, his eyes tried to focus. I think he saw me, just for a second. I thought I saw an attempted smile. And then he was gone. I saw the life physically leave him, but I refused to believe it.

"No," I screamed at the top of my voice. "No, no, no." I repeated looking up towards the heavens. I shook his head to try to wake him. Why had he fallen asleep?

I tried to get to my feet. My intention was to drag him away to safety, to go back down the hill the way we had come. If I could reach the house with the old couple by the river maybe the woman would be able to look after him and he might make a full recovery.

I tried to heave him upwards to his feet, but with only one arm it was too difficult, and I fell back down immediately. I tried again with the same result, and then I felt hands upon me. Someone pulled me away from my friend and held me apart. I tried to free myself from the man's grip, but he was far stronger than me. Another man was kneeling beside Jack, he touched the fingers of his hand to his neck and then looked at me and shook his head. He said something which I did not understand.

"Inglés," I told him.

"Amigos, comrades," he said apologetically. It took a bit for it to sink in, but eventually I realised that we had been shot at by our own side. As Brigadistas we didn't wear the same uniform as the Spanish Republican troops. In fact, there was no official uniform for the International Brigades, there was a sort of anything goes policy. We stole a lot from the dead of both sides, and many wore clothes from their own countries. And it was dusk, and nobody could have expected any of our side to still be at large in the Aragon. We had been taken for the Fascist advanced scouts that these men had been expecting to see all day.

I let the men lead me to their position in a trench just by the road. They sat me down on a rock and one of them started pulling at my shirt to look at my wound. It was strange, but I hadn't yet felt any real pain, just a numbness all down that side of my body. I heard other man chatting casually, one offered me a drag of his cigarette. I shook my head.

The man attending to my injury mopped up most of the blood and then produced a small glass bottle of some clear liquid. He unscrewed the cap and poured a generous measure over the wound. It burned like hell and I shouted out in pain. Now I felt like I'd been shot all right.

I began to sob. From the pain, from the feeling of being terrified and, most of all, for my dead friend. Now I was alone. I was alone in a foreign country. I was wounded, but most of all I was alone. And terrified. My left arm was bandaged and put into a sling and this eased the pain slightly.

I was given some water to drink and then I was helped upright and led back towards the road where a donkey and cart were waiting. Jack's body had already been loaded onto the back and I was pushed up to sit beside him. A local man, old as the hills, was sitting at the front of the cart and cracked a whip to set the animal in motion. The donkey appeared to be just as old as its owner and plodded off slowly.

It was a terrible journey, bouncing along the uneven road, every jolt making my wound hurt more until I closed my eyes to the pain and just let my body sway to and fro with the ship-like motion of the cart. With my eyes closed I could no longer see Jack's face, and I was glad of that. I had failed him, and he was gone. And the terrible thing was, his death had made absolutely no difference to the world whatsoever. The only one who would miss him was me. I think at that moment, on the back of that lurching donkey cart, I hoped that I would die too. I had certainly never felt so alone.

*

Mercifully, it wasn't a long journey. I felt the cart climb another small hill and then we began to descend. I opened my eyes and managed to turn just enough to look at the road ahead. I could see that we were nearing a town. It wasn't a big place, just a group of stone houses clustered around a hill, dominated by a huge church. The spire was different from any I had seen on my trek across the Aragon, it appeared to be octagonal and was flat across the top, not pointed like an English church spire or rounded with decorative tiles as I had seen in other towns that we had passed through. There were old defensive walls too, which showed that this had once been a stronghold, probably back in medieval times, but these walls, crumbling as they were, would be no match for Franco's rampaging advance once it arrived. And arrive it would, at any moment.

"Batea?" I asked the old man up front.

"Sí, Batea," he mumbled back, nodding his head.

Somehow, against all odds, I had arrived in Batea. However, I didn't feel proud of myself. I wouldn't have made it without Walt and Jack. I would have just curled myself up in one of those isolated shepherd's shelters and slept myself to death rather than have surrendered to the enemy. Surrender meant death anyway, that had been drummed into us right from our first moments in Spain.

We approached a roadblock at the entrance to the town, but we weren't stopped. The two young soldiers there just stood aside and let us through. Then, the donkey struggled up the slope towards the centre. There was a big square with stone porticoes, a lazy fountain in the middle, trees around the edges. The war seemed a million miles away. There were people coming and going from the narrow streets that gave onto the square, some were in uniform, some were not. There was a woman pushing a pram. It didn't seem real to me. Didn't she know that the Rebel army was on its way? Didn't she know that Caspe, the last town in the Aragon was now in Fascist hands? How far could it be from Caspe to Batea I wondered? Not far probably, and the Fascists would not walk across country, go on a detour to a non-existent fuel dump or follow a winding river. They would pile into lorries and charge along the road with the speed of wild horses. In fact, it amazed me that they hadn't arrived here before me.

On the far side of the square, was a house that had been turned into a makeshift hospital and this is where the old man decided I should be left. He helped me inside and handed me over to a nurse and asked what he should do with the body in the back of his cart. The woman just shrugged, took hold of my good arm and led me into the interior of the house.

I was seen by a doctor with little round glasses who quickly removed my bandages, inspected my arm and gave a nod of approval. He said something to the nurse and left.

The nurse cleaned my wound with another dose of the clear liquid that burned like hell and bandaged it up once more. She sat me down in an old armchair in an interior patio and gestured for me to stay there. I leaned back in the chair and promptly fell asleep.

I was awoken a while later by a gentle tug on my right arm. It was the same nurse. She held out a bowl of stew with a spoon sticking out of it. Forgetting my manners, I snatched it from her and wolfed it down in under a minute. She looked on in amazement. Obviously, she had never seen a man on the edge of starvation before. I remembered the piece of chorizo that Jack had made me save, and when the nurse took away the empty bowl, I ate that too.

When the nurse returned once more, she led me up a flight of narrow stairs to the first floor where there were mattresses spread out on the floor. It was a big room and through an open door it linked to another of about the same size which again had mattresses. There were men lying on most of them. Some were asleep or unconscious, most were lying on their backs staring up at the ceiling. No one looked at me as the nurse led me through to the far room.

She pointed to an empty space in the far corner.

"Rest," she said in English and gave a small smile. I sat down on the mattress and went about removing my boots. Then I lay down on my right side facing the wall, covered myself with the thin blanket that had been provided and fell asleep.

During the night, I awoke at regular intervals. I wasn't used to sleeping on a mattress, albeit a lumpy straw-filled one, and if I tried to move, my arm hurt. In fact, it ached and throbbed so much that I began to worry that it might need to be amputated. What then? Well, I would have to be shipped back to England for sure. Maybe this wound was a lifesaver, my ticket out of this hell. But, when I got back to England, what then? I wouldn't be able to go back to work on the building site that was for sure.

The next time I was awake was because someone in the other room started screaming. I heard a nurse try to calm him, but he went on screaming for a long time. Eventually, her soothing tone did the trick and there was quiet once more.

During other moments of wakefulness, I would desperately try not to cry. In my mind, in the darkness, I could picture Jack's face as I held it in my hands and looked down upon him. If I had been a better soldier, or a better friend, I might have been able to save him. If I had walked ahead of him on the road, and not behind like a coward, I would have been able to take the bullet instead of him.

Morning came at last, daylight coming in through a gap in the shutters. I kept my face turned to the wall and feigned sleep. I had no desire for anyone to try to engage in conversation with me. I was frustrated and fed up with not being able to speak the language and I just wanted to go back to England. My reason for coming to Spain had been to be with Jack and now he was gone and therefore I could see no reason to remain. I wondered if I could find someone with the power to get me sent home, but who would have that power?

Breakfast was a tin mug of something warm and brown that I guessed was supposed to be coffee and a small piece of sawdust-tasting bread. I dipped the bread into the foul liquid and waited for it to get soft enough to eat. Around mid-morning, the nurse came to look at me. She helped me to my feet and led me downstairs to see the doctor. My bandage was removed, and the doctor watched as the nurse cleaned it once more. In the meantime, he was filling out a form with details of my wound. It was a series of tick boxes that no doubt made things more efficient.

"Name?" he asked me in English.

"Billy," I said. "Billy Bird." He wrote it down on the top of the form and next to it I saw him put Brigadista inglés. The nurse looked at what he had written.

"Pájaro?" she asked. I didn't understand. She turned her face upwards and chirped like a bird.

"Yes, Bird."

She laughed and even the doctor smiled. Once my wound was re-bandaged, she took me to the patio, and I sat once more in an armchair. Over the course of the next hour or so, more men were brought down and dumped into armchairs in the patio. We could hear someone cleaning upstairs. I remember looking around at the other men, all of whom seemed in a worse state than me, but none of whom had life-threatening injuries. It must be a sort of convalescence home I figured. Somewhere where they brought the lightly wounded until they were ready to return to the front line.

It was then, in that patio with it's a hundred-year-old armchairs and its fading geraniums in pots in the corners, that I realised that Spain wasn't finished with me yet.

Lunch was the same stew that I had eaten the day before, but that didn't bother me in the slightest. The nurse handed me the bowl and called me "Pájarito." Little Bird. She was old enough to be my mother. Maybe she had sons fighting away on some other front or maybe they were lost in the Aragon, or maybe they were just dead.

After lunch, my fellow patients dropped into a siesta coma. I leant my head back and tried to sleep too, but before I could I heard boots enter the patio from the direction of the street.

"Bird?" someone asked in an English voice.

I opened my eyes. I raised my right hand to signal my presence.

"Ah, there you are lad. Sorry not to 'ave come sooner. Been busy you know."

He looked around for an empty armchair and then pulled it over to sit beside me. He had my medical form in his hand and was busy trying to make some sense of it.

"How are doing?" he asked.

"Al'right," I mumbled.

"Are they feeding you."

"Yes."

"That's good then."

"So, William um, Bird. British Battalion. Fifteenth Brigade. Tell me what 'appened to you. They said you just showed up yesterday, out of nowhere."

And so, I told him my story, briefly since I didn't talk much back then. I told him that I had been at Belchite, and about the long trek to Caspe. I told him how three of us had been sent to blow up a non-existent fuel dump and how we had stumbled across some Fascists in an abandoned farmhouse. He took out a small notebook and wrote down the names of first Walt Stevens and then Jack Jackson when I told him they had been killed. I didn't know it at the time, but later, I realised that that interview was a lot more serious than I took it for at the time. The man was a Commissar, sent to check me out, just as they checked up on all of those who had disappeared and then miraculously come back from the dead. Had I been a deserter? Was my wound self-inflicted? Was there even the remotest possibility that I was a Fascist spy or saboteur? If there were even the slightest doubt in his mind then I would just disappear, as so many had done already.

He took my Communist Party membership card away with him and promised to return the next day. In the meantime, I was to rest and not to worry about anything. The British Battalion was there to look after me he said.

"A new shirt would be nice," I told him as he stood up to leave.

"Of course, I'll see what can be done comrade." And he was gone, and I closed my eyes and leant my head back against the armchair and went to sleep just like the rest of the wounded soldiers in there around me. I hadn't asked about the progress of the war or about how it was possible that the Fascists hadn't yet taken Batea, I guess I just didn't give a damn.

CHAPTER SIXTEEN

I could have stayed in that temporary hospital or convalescence home, whatever it was supposed to be, for the rest of my life. I had never felt so safe, never been so well-fed, never had so much rest at any other time of my life.

The commissar returned the following afternoon and pulled up a chair alongside me in the patio once more. He handed me a crumpled grey shirt.

"It was all I could find," he said apologetically, it probably wasn't my size, but at least there wasn't a hole in the arm with a big patch of dried blood around it. I stood and took off my old shirt right there in front of him, moving my left arm carefully as it still ached. The man helped me pull the new shirt into place and do up the buttons down the front. I felt like a new man.

"Thanks," I mumbled.

"So, Billy, your story seems to check out. I assume that the Jack Jackson you refer to is Brian Jackson from London, age nineteen. Am I right?"

"Brian?"

"Yes, we have no Jack Jackson. It must have been his nickname."

"I guess," I responded with a shrug. To me he had always been Jack.

"Anyway, I'm 'ere to get you discharged and take you back to the barracks. You'll be right as rain in a few days, you'll see. We need every man we've got in case Franco swings this way."

"Why ain't 'e come already?" I asked.

"Seems to want his troops to get a breather, with any luck then he'll try to push through to the sea," was the reply. So rather than push on into Catalunya, Franco seemed to have decided to reach the Mediterranean. Even I knew that meant the Republican Zone would be split into two. It was a disaster for the legitimate government, but it would at least buy us some much-needed time to regroup to defend Catalunya. Now perhaps Britain and France might realise just how drastic the situation was and finally come to the Republic's aid, before it was too late.

"What happened to Jack's body?" I asked.

"I guess it got taken to the fosa común, the communal grave," said the Commissar. "All the bodies get taken there." He said it without any emotion, like he didn't care at all, and of course he didn't. The only one who cared was me.

I hated to picture Jack's body being tossed into a common pit on top of a pile of other bodies, it just didn't seem right. I swallowed deeply and tried not to cry.

"Right, now then, get your things and let's go."

I went back upstairs and retrieved my belt and ammunition pouches. I didn't have anything else. I smiled a goodbye smile to the nurse who gave me a little wave and said "adios Pájarito."

And then we were out in the street. The brightness was blinding after so long in the shuttered hospital. The commissar marched me across the square, past the now dead fountain to the porticoed area at the far end. We headed along a narrow street, climbing slightly uphill. At last we came to an elegant building that had become our temporary barracks.

Once inside, my paperwork was handed over to a Captain and the Commissar disappeared. The Captain said he was glad that I had found my way back to Batea. He told me that numbers were terribly depleted, although there were still a few odds and sods turning up in ones and twos. He didn't know how they did it quite frankly. Of the six hundred who had gone into the battle of Teruel only twenty remained, he told me with a sad smile. Anyway, it was good that I was safe.

He gave me my party card and told me that someone would show me my space and that my rifle was there. I'd forgotten about my rifle. I hadn't thought I would ever need it again. So, I wasn't going to be sent home. Spain hadn't finished with me yet. I still had the possibility of dying for the cause. Maybe that would be for the best, it would stop me having to feel guilty about what had happened for the rest of my life.

At least, I had escaped from the Aragon something that at times I never thought I would. And I prayed never to return. However, as much as I might be finished with the Aragon, the Aragon wasn't finished with me quite yet.

*

My wound was just a flesh wound, the bullet had nicked my arm but not entered it. I had been lucky. I was a living testament to our side's poor armaments or poor training or both. I went back to the hospital in the square to let the doctor have another look at my arm, but he was satisfied that everything was healing well. At last, I was able to remove the dressing and let the fresh air get at it. I would always have a scar. It would be a permanent reminder of my time in Spain and I would never be able to look at it without thinking of my friend Jack. I missed him so badly. And I think that the world would have been a better place had he lived a full life, and I don't just mean that from a selfish point of view. Who knows what he might have made of his life? A businessman, a politician or just a family man working in a factory. All possibilities had been taken from him.

My survival story from the Battle of the Aragon was by no means unique. Miraculously, there were still others turning up, men who had been given up for lost and had somehow made it to safety. The people of the Aragon might have been forced to change sides as they were absorbed into the ever-expanding Nationalist zone, but their hearts were still loyal to the Republic. They helped lost soldiers as best they could, often giving shelter and food at a terrible risk to themselves and their families.

In Batea, we slowly began to recover. We washed and shaved every day. We scrounged new items of uniform where we could. I guessed that most of the new shirts and trousers and boots came from dead men. But they had no use for these things now, and they meant a lot to those of us who had been lucky enough to survive. It was late March, and the weather was starting to get warmer by the day. I had heard tales of the unbearable heat of summer, and I wasn't looking forward to it. How were you supposed to fight a war with temperatures nearly double what you would find in England? The retreat across the Aragon had been hard enough in late winter, with temperatures at times like an English summer, I couldn't begin to imagine what it would have been like in the summer. I for one wouldn't have made it. I'm sure many others wouldn't have either, especially the Brigadistas from colder climates.

We were permitted to wander around the town in the evenings, although not in large groups and we were sworn to be on our best behaviour. No drunkenness. No whoring. No fighting with our Spanish comrades. We were even given money to spend. This took the form of tiny tickets printed on cream-coloured card. They said: Ajuntament de Batea. Val Una Pesseta. We were in Catalunya, hence the spelling of peseta and Ajuntament instead of Ayuntamiento. However, the money meant nothing. There was nothing to buy. At least nothing to buy for one peseta. There was a thriving black market though and groups of men pooled their tickets together and blew the lot on a rancid bottle of wine or an ancient tin of sardines. I put mine in my pocket and there it stayed.

At least we were fed regularly. For me, that was the best thing about Batea. And the chance to sleep inside. Our makeshift barracks was crowded and smelly but, sure beat sleeping out in the fields. At night, as I lay awake listening to the booming snores of my companions, I would think back to the night that jack and I had spent in that stone shepherd's shelter. The cierzo raging all around and the lightning making our faces look like the faces of demons.

It turned out, when a final tally was taken, that the XV Brigade had lost over a thousand men killed, missing or wounded in the futile battle to save the

Aragon. The XI and XIII Brigades, also of the 35th Division, had suffered just as much. Along with the 45th Division we were the ones who had faced the might of the Nationalist war machine as it drove on, like a knife through butter, towards the coast. We had faced a far superior enemy, aided by Italian tanks and aircraft and of course the dreaded German Stukas. Add to that the accuracy of the Rebel artillery, their vastly superior weaponry and the Army of Africa, and it was no surprise that there had been a rout. The miracle of the Aragon was that any of us had survived. And so, we regrouped, the XV Brigade at Batea, licked our wounds and waited to see how long this fragile respite would last.

*

On March 26th, after almost a week in Batea we suddenly left. We were transferred in lorries to the little town of Corbera d'Ebre. We passed through the high ground of the Coll del Moro, the sharp mountain peaks cutting up into the clouds, the lorries straining with all their might to get us through to Gandesa. From there it wasn't far to Corbera d'Ebre.

The town was huddled on top of a hill with a commanding view of the surrounding countryside. Somewhere away to the east, was the mighty River Ebro, but it was hidden from view by the heights of the Serra de Cavalls. We were in a little pocket of land left as the Ebro took the easy route, skirting the high ground of the Serra de la Fatarella, Serra de Cavalls and the Serra de Pandols. We had no idea of course at that time just how important that little area was going to become in what remained of the war.

Corbera was a small town, with a population of around three thousand, made up of low stone houses that blended into the folds of the hill up from the main road. Its most remarkable feature, in common with most Spanish towns and villages I had seen, was the church. The church of Sant Pere. It stood on a piece of flat land, just as the hill passed its peak on the eastern side, its tall square tower built in two stages, topped by a triangular roof, dominating the skyline.

The area to the right of the main road from Gandesa was farmland in long thin fields enclosed by neat stone walls and planted mostly with small fruit trees. I don't think that these people would ever have imagined that soldiers from so many different parts of the world would suddenly descend on their sleepy town, but the International Brigades had arrived. It must have been strange for them to hear unfamiliar languages other than their normal everyday Català. The local people crowded onto their balconies to watch as we marched up through the streets to find our barracks. They cheered and clapped and thought we were there to save them, but we weren't.

Those few days at Corbera d'Ebre passed quietly. We had political meetings in a variety of languages, all of which I sat through and totally ignored, even the ones in English meant nothing to me. My whole reason for being in Spain had gone with the death of my friend. Now, all I wanted to do was get through to the end of the war which surely couldn't be too far away. Having said that, the thought of returning to England without Jack was not a pleasant one. I guess there was the possibility that I could go back to our old lodgings. I could imagine the widow with whom we had boarded breaking down into hysterical floods of tears at the news of Jack's death. Had she really loved him? I'm not sure, but I liked to think that she would be saddened to hear of his death, they had after all been as close as it was possible for two people to be. Maybe she would take me into her bed some nights as a ready-made replacement for her dead lover, and maybe I would get larger portions of dinner in return like Jack had done. I would look for a job in a factory rather than a building site I decided, I hated those cold winter mornings outside.

Four days we stayed in Corbera d'Ebre. When I could, I would slip away from the barracks after the day's activities had finished. We cleaned and mended weapons and discussed tactics on a little field just outside of town, at the back of the hill from where the houses were. I liked to wander slowly around the narrow streets looking at the people of the town trying as best they could to carry on with their normal everyday lives. The women would fetch water from the fountain or take baskets of washing down to the little river just beyond the main road, to wash and hang out their clothes and sheets to dry on the bushes. There were no young men around except for us soldiers. The young men from the town were mostly already dead in the service of the Republic, and those who remained alive had probably been taken to the larger cities of Catalunya to prepare for the next stage of the war. No one believed it was possible to halt the Nationalist advance this side of the Ebro, but maybe the great river would serve as a natural barrier that could protect Catalunya for a while. That of course meant that this little area on the wrong bank would soon be abandoned.

The narrow streets offered shade in the afternoons now that the days were getting warmer. I would work my way downwards towards the Carrer Major, dodging other Brigadistas or old men with donkeys, and continue on through the arched entrance to the main Gandesa highway, and then I would turn and head back to make sure I was back in time for tea.

Food was better than normal. The local smallholders must have thought it a good idea to sell their surplus produce to the Republican army rather than wait for the Nationalist army to arrive and steal it. The little tickets printed by the town council that served as money here, however, were unlikely to be accepted once the Rebels arrived.

On the Tuesday morning, after four days of relative calm we received the news that we would be returning to battle. Franco had resumed his push towards the Mediterranean. We were given short notice to get our kit together, and then we marched out of town. The people once more crowded their balconies to see us go. This time they weren't cheering. It was obvious that we were leaving them to their fate. They looked down at us as we passed beneath them, their faces etched with worry. Some of the women were crying. A few small boys gathered just beyond the archway out of town to wave us off, not understanding what lay in store for them now.

As for us, to our great surprise, we were told that we were heading back into the Aragon one last time. Who would have imagined that there might still be a tiny part of the Aragon left to fight over? Our destination was a little place called Calaceite. The name meant nothing to me of course, upon first hearing it, but it was a name I would never be able to forget for the rest of my life.

CHAPTER SEVENTEEN

We marched along the main road to Gandesa, where we drank water at a fountain and refilled our personal bottles before a food truck arrived from Corbera d'Ebre. We sat in the shade of some trees in a little square, set back from the main road and ate and rested for a bit. And then we were off again. I wondered why we had to walk, probably there weren't enough lorries for a whole division, or most likely there wasn't enough fuel.

After a brief rest, we were on our way again. It was about twenty miles from Corbera d'Ebre to Calaceite, and we were needed there urgently. From Gandesa, the road climbed up through the Serra dels Pesells towards the Coll del Moro. There was an old Iberian settlement with the remains of a stone tower towards the summit. I hadn't seen it when we had come past by lorry previously from Batea.

It was an exhausting afternoon as we climbed ever upwards. I didn't think that when we arrived in Calaceite we would be in any kind of condition to fight a battle.

From the Coll del Moro the road just took us on towards the next hill to climb, which if anything appeared to be even higher. After a couple of hours, maybe three, we came to the crossroads where the road between Batea and Bot crossed ours. I remembered the few days I had spent in Batea and wished I could be back there now. It was as if the rest I had enjoyed there had never happened, my body felt just as weary as it had done during the days and nights spent escaping from Belchite. At least this time we were walking along a road, although of course that left us open to attack by enemy aircraft. Especially now that we were out of the cover of the pine forests of the Coll del Moro.

Instead of taking the road to Batea, as I would have liked, we continued along the main Gandesa to Alcañiz road. We forced ourselves over the final climb of the day, and at last we began to descend. There was a little village in sight, just a few ramshackle stone dwellings of a single storey. At first, I thought it was Calaceite, and I began to ask myself why somewhere so insignificant should warrant our protection. But as we got nearer, it became obvious that this couldn't be our destination. It was nestled down in a little river valley that ran between some small hills.

We passed quickly through that village, out of Catalunya and back into the Aragon. It was just beyond the last houses that we heard the unmistakeable drone of approaching aircraft. We scattered, running for our lives. Some set off back to the village, others just ran across country to try to find some cover. The important thing was to get off the road. Now the marching into battle made sense. Had we been in lorries we would all have been blown to hell. I kept running until I judged that the nearest plane was almost on top of me and then threw myself to the ground. I hadn't found anywhere to shelter, not even a rock to hide behind and I had never felt so exposed in all my life. I curled up into a ball and tried to bury my head in my arms. All the while expecting to hear the chatter of guns or the whistling of a bomb.

The next thing I remember was the increase in noise as the plane pulled itself up out of its dive and began to climb away from the road. I kept my head hidden in my hands for quite some time, wondering if the bomb had some sort of delay or something. Maybe it was just a dud and I had been incredibly lucky.

The seconds passed, and no explosion came. In fact, there were no explosions at all. The sound of the aircraft faded right away. Cautiously, I peered up at the sky. It was raining pieces of paper rather than bullets. Nationalist propaganda leaflets. I picked myself up and dusted down my shirt and trousers. All around me, other men were doing the same thing, and all the while white leaflets fluttered down upon us like dying butterflies.

I walked back to the road. Had the pilots carried bombs rather than paper, then I would surely have been blown to pieces. It served as a stark reminder, if one were needed, that in this modern type of war you were never more than a moment away from death.

Someone plucked a falling leaflet out of the air to see what it said.

"They want us to surrender boys!" he shouted gleefully waving the leaflet above his head in an excited manner. "Says we'll be treated fairly."

We all groaned at his false enthusiasm. Nobody was going to fall for that, what a laugh. What a waste of paper but thank god they had sent paper and not bombs. In a couple of minutes, those planes could have wiped out the lot of us.

Once we were all back in position on the road, we marched on. It was late afternoon, and we were tired. We had also just had the scare of our lives. I drank a little water to calm my nerves and to steady my heartbeat. My new grey shirt was filthy with dirt.

About an hour after the false attack by Nationalist planes, we were finally able to see our destination in the distance. There was a stumpy bald hill standing above the village which hugged its lower slopes. The buttressed church had a two-stage tower with a roof that looked like a dome. It was almost the same height as the tower. The houses were mostly brown, but some stood out because they had whitewashed fronts. The roof tiles were the same red/brown that we always saw. Just another typical little village in the Aragon.

Being back in the Aragon made me feel decidedly uneasy, as if something bad was going to happen. It was a place I had hoped I would never see again, and now I was back. This time however, I didn't have Walt and Jack by my side. I tried to fit in with the rest of the Brigade, I really did, they were nearly all older than me. And anyway, I'd seen that it didn't really pay to have friends. You just felt lousy when they were killed. Having said that, I would have given anything to have Jack back at my side.

And the others didn't trust me, not like Walt had. I had changed back from being a soldier into a frightened kid, at least in their eyes. The good thing was that I wasn't trusted enough to be put on watch duty at night. That was something Walt had always trusted me with. He said I had the sharpest eyes and I never once fell asleep on watch.

We made camp in a field just outside of Calaceite, without going into the town itself. Just after dark, a soldier arrived with some donkeys laden with food and we crowded quickly around to get our share. There was always the worry that there wouldn't be enough for everyone and yet there nearly always was. Even so, no one wanted to be last in the queue.

Large white beans, slightly warm and very greasy. At least we would be going to bed on a full stomach. I settled down in the darkness, my back against a cold stone wall at the edge of the field and looked up at the sky. There were thick rolling clouds, grey and forbidding and I wondered if it was going to rain, or worse still, if there was going to be a thunderstorm. After a while I lay down, wrapped up tight in my blanket and my head on my backpack.

I did wonder if this was going to be my last night on earth. It could well be. In the morning, we would be thrown into battle, and none of us had any hope that we might win. The Rebel war machine had shown itself to be far superior in the Aragon. We might be brave, almost foolhardy at times, but it was no match for what Franco could throw at us. We had little ammunition, no grenades, no artillery and no air-support. It had all the makings of a massacre. If I prayed for one thing that long last night, it was that the end, when it came would be swift and painless.

*

We were awoken before dawn to make ourselves ready to move forward. We were to take up a defensive position on the far side of the town, to try to prevent the enemy entering Calaceite. I knew what that meant, that we were the ones who were going to feel the brunt of the Rebel attack.

Just before it was daylight, we were on the move, leaving our makeshift camp without breakfast. Some were grumbling about that. How could we be sent into battle without so much as a biscuit? I was glad though. I had a terrible feeling of nausea forming in the pit of my stomach, and had I eaten anything I might well have been sick. I had shivered all through the night and now I was sweating, and the sun wasn't even up. I wondered if I had caught a chill. Still, what did that matter? You didn't need to be fully fit to be cannon fodder. I just really wanted it to be over with as soon as possible.

From the field where we had spent the night, we marched down the road towards the town. Calaceite was silent, still slumbering, unaware. The shuttered windows of the closest houses still asleep. Most of the population would already have fled towards Mora d'Ebre or Xerta, anywhere where they could cross the Ebro. Those who stayed behind were either stupid, infirm, elderly or eager to betray their Republic and welcome the Fascist conquerors with open arms. The most prominent Loyalists who remained, must have gone to bed knowing that it would be their last night.

Anyone thought to have been an active Republican supporter would be shot as soon as the town was taken. The mayor, any members of the town council, any members of a cooperative or of a trade union like the CNT. Reprisals would be swift and merciless. Mistakes would be made. They always were. No one would care.

We made our way into the town, waking stray dogs as we went, our boots ringing out on the cobbles. I thought it fitting that the first street name I saw was Calle Cierzo. There were no civilians to be seen. When we reached the Plaza de España we paused in the square in front of the archways of the townhall. There seemed to be some confusion as to where exactly we should be going.

Eventually, someone who thought they were in charge emerged from one of the backstreets. Maybe we had always been supposed to meet him there and he had just overslept. He came with five burly soldiers weighed down with ammunition belts. It was like he had personal bodyguards.

The sky was starting to lighten, and dawn was nearly upon us. After much excited chatter between the Brigade leaders and this new arrival, it was obviously decided that he knew what we were supposed to do. In the end, one of the Battalion commanders found our Captain and made it clear to him that the British would take the lead. We were to go with our new Spanish comrade, and he would lead us all into position. Once we were sure of where we were supposed to be and that it was a reasonable position to try to hold, then the rest of the Brigade would follow on. We should send word.

We headed off down the Calle San Antonio, turned right onto the Calle Sagrado Corazón and finally reached the main road out of Calaceite heading towards Alcañiz. It was just about daybreak. I remember the sky was a thousand different colours, none of which I had ever seen before. It was almost as if my brain wanted to absorb as much of what was around me as possible. Were these really to be my last moments on earth? I thought of Jack and imagined some sort of heaven where we might be reunited. He would be waiting there to show me around, to watch my back as he always had done. God I just wanted to get it over with.

We hadn't gone far out of the town, less than a mile I would say. We were strung out in two columns, one on each side of the road. I was towards the front on the left-hand side. As we marched, I looked to cover my side of the road, as did all of those around me. We carried our rifles at the ready pointing out away from us. We were walking through an area of market gardens where local smallholders would have grown things to sell at the weekly market, tomatoes and peppers, potatoes, onions those sort of things. I didn't think any threat would come from there. The danger lay up ahead along the road or in the sky above us as daylight came.

Out of the area of market gardens, we were into the hills. The road snaked out of sight to the right around behind the first hill and there was a scattering of old abandoned farm buildings at the bottom of the slope.

We had just passed them, when suddenly we heard the deafening roar of engines and then around the corner from behind the hill, came a whole armoured column. At first, we thought they must be our troops, but then we saw tanks. The Republic didn't have any tanks in the Aragon, or at least I hadn't seen any. From their uniforms they weren't Spanish troops that was for sure. It all happened so quickly that everyone was just sort of stunned.

"Manos arriba!" came the shout from somewhere, and then it was taken up by others. They weren't Spanish however, and when they jostled us and pushed us into the middle of the road they shouted at us angrily in their own language.

"Italians," I heard someone up ahead shout and then he tried to make a run for it, away from the road up the hillside. He was shot in the back and fell to the ground. That put everyone on edge, and the Italians began to look as if they might slaughter us all. Those who had been towards the rear of the column were able to turn and run back towards the town, able to save themselves. But those of us who had been towards the front were trapped.

I turned to look back in the direction of Calaceite, the sun was now just coming up, and I could see the road back to the town was filled with escaping soldiers. More Italian troops were emerging from the abandoned stone buildings, firing at those who were fleeing. A couple were hit. We had walked into a trap.

A shot rang out startling me, and I turned to see what was happening. A commissar had been shot in the head by an Italian captain and lay on the road in a growing puddle of blood and brains. As I watched, the Spanish officer who had been leading us into position was also shot at close range. His legs simply buckled under him and he fell with a thud as he hit the ground. Those who had been around him, his five bodyguards laden with ammunition belts, backed away leaving him, in case they were to be next. The same officer passed amongst us looking for other officers and commissars. Our captain knew what was coming and suddenly turned to try to run back to Calaceite. He didn't know, like I did, that the way back was now blocked. The soldiers who were walking towards us from the outbuildings shot him down and he died in a hail of bullets. Another man was also hit and doubled up clutching his stomach, blood running out from between his fingers.

At any minute, I expected the officer to give the order to fire and kill the lot of us.

CHAPTER EIGHTEEN

Eventually, amid much shouting and pushing, the Italians forced us towards the stone buildings at the bottom of the hill. We were then crowded into what might have been pigsties or goat pens but now had no roofs. We were left there under guard.

We sat on the floor, huddled together, feeling miserable. Our guards smoked and laughed. Occasionally, one of them would take out a salami or a chorizo and slowly eat it in front of us. It was as if they knew we had been thrown into battle with no breakfast. Still, we had more important things than food to worry about. It looked for all the world like we were going to be shot, and I for one wished they'd just get on with it.

All through that long morning of the last day of March, the battle for Calaceite raged on. We could imagine the other battalions of our brigade fighting heroically, perhaps suicidally, but being forced slowly to give up ground. It would have been house to house, as it had been in Belchite. This attempted defence of Calaceite had been shown to be a real waste of manpower. It would have been far more sensible to retreat across the Ebro, blow the bridges and give the army time to lick its wounds. The Republic, whatever the commissars tried to tell us, could not hope to win this war. Not now. Not now that the Aragon had been lost and Franco had almost completed his drive to the Mediterranean. Soon, Catalunya would be cut off from the rest of the Loyalist zone. So what hope was there? What reason could there be to keep fighting? Well, they might hope to negotiate a peace with Franco and save what territory they had left. It was highly unlikely that Franco would bother to do that with the conquest of the whole of Spain within his grasp. Then there was the forlorn hope that England and France would suddenly end the farce of non-intervention and come to the aid of the legitimate Spanish government. But that of course would plunge Europe into a much larger war that no one wanted. The third option was to keep fighting in the hope that a global war did break out, and that Republican Spain could become part of a more widespread fight against Fascism. The final option I could think of was the most likely one; that the Republic would just keep fighting because there was nothing else it could do. Complete surrender was unthinkable, imagine the reprisals in places like Madrid and Barcelona. Complete surrender could lead to the wholesale slaughter of large proportions of the population in those areas that had held out to the end. But the death of the Republic seemed now like a foregone conclusion.

For us at least, the struggle was over. For us there were only two options that I could make out. Be shot en masse or sent to a prison camp. I wasn't sure that the Nationalists had prisoner of war camps. It had been so well drummed into us that they didn't take prisoners, that it was easy to believe that no such thing existed on their side of the lines. So why then hadn't we already been shot? One of the men came up with the theory that the Italians didn't want to shoot us without direct orders to do so, seeing as we were mostly British. Would Franco or for that matter Mussolini really want to anger Great Britain by committing such a dreadful deed against her citizens? A mass killing might mean the end of non-intervention and Britain's support for the Republic.

So, we sat there in those abandoned pigsties through into the afternoon, moving around as best we could to keep in the areas of shade as the sun reached its highest point. Our guards gave up standing watching us with rifles at the ready and instead sat in the shade of a gloomy-looking fig tree and smoked and drank wine from those leather pouches that the locals used. The noise of the battle for Calaceite was slowly receding. It seemed for all the world that we had been forgotten about.

By mid-afternoon, the battle seemed to have ended. We saw a plane pass overhead but heard no bombs. I wondered if any of our brigade had managed to survive. We had become masters in fighting a retreat, so there was always hope. That a lot of men had been lost was beyond doubt. We had taken hit after hit in the last month and numbers were becoming depleted and resources had reached the breaking point. It was a testament to the strength of the men's convictions that there hadn't been mass desertions.

A little while after the battle seemed to have finished, the shooting began. Volleys of gunfire that indicated that the firing squads were in full swing. At the first volley we all looked at each other. Nothing was said, there was no need. Our faces showed the fear. Then we heard the unmistakeable sound of approaching motor vehicles.

We were shepherded back out onto the road and made to line up. There were members of the Civil Guard there who had come with the lorries. That's what the Italians had been waiting for, to pass us and therefore any responsibility for our safety over to them. The officer in charge of the Civil Guard began to shout. One of our men who spoke the language began to interpret what was required.

"Any of you who are Jews, Communists, Socialists or machine-gunners should take a step forward now."

My heart skipped a beat. I had been a machine-gunner and I had a Communist Party membership card in my shirt pocket.

"On the count of three we all step forward," decided our interpreter. He was right of course, all of us were at least one of those things, some were more than one. I wondered if they could tell if you had been a machine-gunner just by looking you in the eyes. The Communist Party membership card was starting to burn a hole in my breast pocket.

On the count of three, we took a collective pace forward. The Civil Guard officer became hysterical waving his pistol in the interpreter's face. His men raised their rifles and pointed them at the chests of anyone they thought might be a threat. Suddenly, the officer backed away and barked some orders at his men. For a second or two, I expected them to open fire and finish us off.

Then, a couple of them approached us and began to turn out pockets and search for documentation. If a Communist Party card was found, you were pushed over to the far side of the road away from the group. Those who were not found to be members of the party were pushed towards the waiting lorries and urged to climb aboard.

My heart began to pound out of control. I felt the urge to cry and felt myself trembling all over.

"Stiff upper lip, Billy lad," whispered the man beside me. I looked at him and he gave me a sad smile. I swallowed and took a deep breath and tried to remain calm. It wasn't easy. The men doing the searching got closer. I felt as if I were going to be sick.

The soldier next to me was searched and his Communist Party card found in his back trouser pocket. He was pushed over to one side. My turn came. I puffed out my chest and tried to look unconcerned. The young civil guard went straight for my left breast pocket and fished out the guilty piece of paper. In Barcelona we had been given Spanish Communist Party cards in exchange for our own CPGB ones. It was stamped with a blue ink stamp that said Partido Comunista de España and left no doubt as to the bearer's political affiliation. It even had a soviet style sickle with a star in the middle. I was given a shove over towards the group that wasn't going to be getting onto the lorries.

When the selection process was done, we watched the lorries drive away. There were shouts of encouragement both ways until the lorries were out of shouting distance. The Civil Guards were gone, and we were left in the hands of the Italian Fascists once more. We were lined up and then we began the march back to Calaceite. It was late afternoon and the sun was beginning to descend.

I saw as we approached, that the town had changed dramatically. A pall of smoke hung over it like a shroud and there were several buildings on fire. Many of the houses had been reduced to ruins and the fine whitewashed façades of the morning were blackened and riddled with bullet holes. It looked like our guys had put up quite a fight, but the greater military might of the Italian Corpo Truppe Volontarie had always been destined to come out on top. Again, it seemed like a terrible waste to me. Was this last little piece of the Aragon really that important?

We marched as slowly as we dared, just to annoy the Italians who were eager to get to their evening meal. They would curse us and threaten to hit us with their rifle buts. And so, we would speed up just a bit. But not for long. The officer in charge carried our Communist Party cards and any other incriminatory evidence in one hand and his pistol in the other.

We entered Calaceite the same way we had left it that morning. It seemed so long ago now. There was a new smell to the place. A pungent mixture of smoke, cordite and blood.

The Plaza de España was a hive of activity. Italian soldiers were rushing about to and fro, ducking in and out of the archways, continually bumping into each other and cursing one another at the tops of their voices. There were also bodies dotted about the square. Some in uniform, some civilians. The shiny stones of the square were slippery with blood. A group of frightened children were huddled under an archway their faces black with grime and smoke. These were the children of those who had been executed or whose houses had been destroyed by the bombing and shelling. I wondered if the Italians felt proud of themselves when they saw these homeless orphans. Some were sobbing, others had already cried themselves out.

The ayuntamiento had a new flag. The red, yellow red striped version having replaced the red, yellow and purple one that had been there that morning. As we arrived, we witnessed a man being dragged out of the townhall forced to kneel on the ground and then shot in the head. The children grouped over on the far side under the archway began screaming, and those who had thought they could cry on more suddenly found they were able to do so. What did they understand of the war? How could they comprehend why someone who their parents had probably known was suddenly being shot in the head in their normally peaceful main square, by soldiers who had come from another country?

We were taken into the town hall. There were bullet holes in the white walls and blood on the tiled floor. We were marched up some stairs to the first floor into the big room where council meetings would have been held in better times. And there we remained, under guard and wondered what our fate might be.

After an age, the commander appeared with a gaggle of men and spoke to the officer who had brought us there. They talked at some length before the officer handed over the identity documents that had been taken from us. We were made to line up against the wall. I was the farthest from the door at the end seeing as I had been cowering at the back of the group.

The Commander, his uniform immaculate like it was brand new, went along the line like some small Caesar. Pausing before each prisoner, he would shuffle through the documents until he found the right one by comparing the photograph to its owner. When he was satisfied that he had the right face, he barked a command to one of his soldiers and the man was removed from the room.

And so, I was the last one left. The Commanding Officer, General, Caesar whatever he might call himself stood there looking at me for a while. I was desperately trying not to cry. I tried to take a deep breath to steady the trembling that I felt all over. Billy, I said to myself, it's time to be a man now. I swallowed deeply and raised my face to look at the man. He was old, older than any soldier I had ever seen. Our leaders were mostly young men who had shown themselves capable of leading the People's Army. Even Franco was only in his mid-forties.

And so, I stood there in the splendour of the council chamber, looking at this old man, trying to make out that I wasn't afraid. I wanted to show him that I would accept my fate as all the others had done. This old man had the power of life and death over me at that moment. For me, he wasn't a General or a Caesar or even a human being – he was a god.

CHAPTER NINETEEN

The Italian went over to the great wooden table around which the local council members had sat for meetings and placed all the identification documents on it. Except one. Mine. He came back towards me and gave a sad smile.

"How old?" he asked.

"Eighteen," I mumbled.

"My grandson is eighteen."

He seemed to think for a while and then having reached a decision, he tore my Communist Party card into pieces and dropped it on the floor. He gave orders to one of his soldiers and I was led away.

Back out in the daylight, in the Plaza de España, the rest of the group were waiting for us. The soldier who was leading me explained what the Commanding Officer had told him to his countrymen, and then we were all led down to a place where there was a sort of reservoir right within the town. This was the Palza de la Balsa. A flight of wide stone steps led down to the water. The level was quite high given that the spring melt was already in progress in the mountains. A soft wind blew ripples across the surface, the sun's last rays reflecting off the water making it shine like liquid gold. At the bottom of the steps there was a wide ledge with a high retaining wall to stop the water overflowing and getting into the streets in times of extreme capacity.

The men were lined up along the wall. I went to take my place, but the soldier who was with me grabbed my arm and pulled me back. I looked at him, he wasn't much older than me. He shook his head quickly and led me back towards the steps. We paused there. I heard commands being given, but it was all like a living nightmare. I couldn't believe what they were about to do. Orders were given in Italian and the soldiers brought their rifles up to their shoulders.

"¡Viva la República!" shouted one of the men.

"Viva," responded the others.

"No," I screamed at the top of my lungs. I closed my eyes. I screwed them up tight and turned away. The order came and a volley of shots rang out like a rolling thunderclap.

Starlings that had been looking to settle down for the night in the trees of the Plaza de la Balsa, suddenly blew into flight, screaming and crying out in alarm. Hundreds of them. The sky was suddenly black with screeching birds, tumbling over each other in their rush to get away. There followed the occasional bullet as one of our men was found to be stubbornly alive. The shots rang out shrill and precise. The young Italian soldier led me the rest of the way up the steps to the square. I didn't look back. I couldn't. It was something I didn't want to see. I was taken to the cuartel where the civil guard had once lived with their families, although there were none there now. I was locked into a tiny prison cell with a small barred window. A straw mattress lay on the floor. I went over to the window and looked out. There was a square, in the middle of which was a fountain for drinking water. A woman was there filling an earthenware jug. It was amazing that life was intent on carrying on after what had happened.

I was given nothing to eat or drink, so I lay down on the mattress and tried to stop thinking about what I had been through. At some stage, alone in the darkness except for the sound of moaning, like a wounded animal, coming from another cell, I must have fallen asleep.

I was constantly troubled by nightmares. Sometimes, I half woke up, cleared my mind as best I could and then I was plunged once more into darkness. I shivered. I sweated. I cried at times. There was still the thought at the back of my mind, that come the morning I would be shot. I know that doesn't make sense. If they wanted to shoot me, they could just have done it down by the balsa. And yet, my mind wasn't thinking straight, how could it?

I had never felt so alone as that night in the calabozo in Calaceite. It was without doubt the longest and most miserable night of my life.

*

Somehow, I made it through to morning. It was early, just daylight when the young Italian soldier came back to check on me. He passed a small piece of bread through the bars of the wooden door to the cell. I stuffed it quickly into my mouth in case it was a mistake and he wanted it back. It was softer than the bread I was used to, and I managed to swallow it down almost whole. The young soldier looked at me in amazement and then laughed. I wondered if it might be part of his own ration.

"Agua," I begged him in Spanish. He understood and seemed to think about it for a moment, and then he nodded his head. He went and found the key to the door and unlocked it and gestured for me to follow him. We went outside into the square and he led me over to the water fountain. There were a couple of women there filling jars and chatting excitedly despite the early hour. It was chilly. We stood waiting for them to finish. The women looked at me with pity. They saw a poor young lad who was probably going to be shot in the next few days. The one who was next in line said something to the one who was filling her jar, and she stood up and gestured for me to have drink.

I didn't refuse the offer. I rushed over and ducked my head down to drink. Just at that moment, there came the roar of approaching aircraft. They were flying low. None of us thought anything of it. I continued drinking. The roar became louder still, almost directly above us. Suddenly I heard the unmistakeable whistle of a falling bomb. I threw myself to the ground behind the stone basin of the fountain.

There was a huge roar, it was as if all the air in the world was suddenly sucked out through a hole in the atmosphere. I felt pressure on my chest and the noise of the explosion so close at hand was deafening. Another explosion followed a little further away. Then there were more that seemed to come from all over Calaceite. I heard the thud of falling bricks onto the stones of the square and stayed low. I dared to glance skywards and saw five aircraft turn and head away from the town.

They were the first Republican planes I had seen over the Aragon. I picked myself up. There was dense smoke covering everything. I was covered in dust from the blast. The two women were dead, and the Italian soldier had been cut in half by the force of the blast. The cuartel was a smoking mass of rubble and fire was licking around the remaining righthand side wall.

I was dazed and half deaf, but I knew that I had been given a chance to escape. I didn't know exactly where I was, but I knew I had to get myself out of town whilst everything was still in a state of confusion. I hurried away from the cuartel along a narrow street that took me downhill slightly and eventually I came to the Plaza de la Balsa. From there, it wasn't far to the edge of town. I pressed on, hurrying but not running so as not to draw attention to myself. I needn't have worried, in all the chaos no one cared about me. Local people were trying to put out fires or frantically digging with their hands in the ruins of houses crying out the names of their children. The bodies of dead Italian soldiers lay all around. And the wounded screamed, and the mothers wailed.

I kept to the fields, away from the road, throwing myself over the walls and dodging in and out of the trees. I saw a camp in the same place that we had spent the night before the battle and realised that all the Italian soldiers were streaming down the road into the town, to help as best they could. I looked back briefly at Calaceite when I was halfway up the first hill. It was covered in a shroud of smoke, so that it was almost invisible. Just the top of the rocky hill around which the town was built, and the tower of the church were visible. No one would have thought that the Republican air force could have mounted such an attack. They had carried it off just at the stroke of dawn before the sky filled with enemy fighters for the day.

I reached the little village not far from Calaceite and was able to wash the worst of the dust out of my hair and ears and nose. Then I rinsed my mouth out with the freezing water to take away the taste of cordite. My ears were still ringing.

I pressed forward keeping as close to the road as I dared, but never walking directly along it. I knew that if I kept the road in sight, then I could follow it back to Gandesa, and that was my only thing I could think of.

After an hour or so, I was starting to feel tired and wished I had a water bottle to fill in the stream where I had stopped before. I didn't stop to rest though. I really wanted to get to Gandesa before nightfall.

As I crested a small hill, I saw the crossroads where the Batea to Bot road ran across the main route that I was following. I wondered what had happened to Batea. Was it still in Loyalist hands? I doubted it, and so I resisted the temptation to head that way. I did wonder what had happened to the little hospital where I had been, probably the Rebels had entered and started shooting everyone. Did they shoot nurses? It was probably best to hope that they did.

As the road dropped down the slope of the hill, so I followed close beside it. I was ready to run and hide amongst the yellow boulders if I heard approaching aircraft. I now knew it was possible to be targeted by your own side as well as the enemy.

As I neared the crossroads, I heard voices. There were men a little way back from the road hidden amongst some boulders. I instantly dropped to the ground on my belly, panting like a frightened animal. I took some deep breaths to calm myself down as much as possible, to let myself think for a second. The best thing to do was to retreat a little and then give the crossroads as wide a berth as possible. I decided I would crawl away as far as I could and then make a run for it crouching as low as I could. I lay there trying to psyche myself up to get moving when I heard the voices again. There was a louder voice and some laughter, then different voices and to my surprise, I realised that they were English.

I couldn't believe my luck. As far as I was aware, there were no Britishers on the Rebel side, so these men had to be those who had managed to escape from the ambush in Calaceite. I stood up and began to approach them.

"Hey, don't shoot comrades," I called out as loudly as I could. "British Battalion."

That was it, about twenty men appeared out of nowhere all pointing guns at me. I threw my hands up into the air to show them I was unarmed.

"It's Billy Bird!" said someone. There was a collective groan of relief.

"Fuck me Billy!" said someone else and they all laughed.

"What happened to you lad?" they wanted to know.

I told them about being taken prisoner and about the firing squad down by the balsa. Everyone went silent.

"Bastards!" someone said at last.

CHAPTER TWENTY

We stayed there throughout the long afternoon, hidden amongst the boulders, hugging their shade, waiting for the Fascists. We didn't know from which direction they would appear first. Would it be the Italians from Calaceite or some other Rebel force from the direction of Batea. Planes flew overhead from time to time, but they didn't spot us. Perhaps they were bombing Gandesa. Maybe the enemy had already managed to cross the Ebro, and they were now bombing the major cities en route to Barcelona such as Lleida or Tarragona.

Personally, I didn't think us staying there at the crossroads was a good idea at all. What were we going to do to halt the unstoppable advance? I reminded the others just how well equipped the Italians were, how they even had tanks, but I was ignored. How could we fight tanks with just our rifles? I didn't even have a rifle for fuck's sake. What was I supposed to do? Throw stones at them? It was suicide to stay there. The others seemed to think that they could hold up the advance and somehow help to save the Republic. I thought they had all gone mad. They hoped their sacrifice would allow the rest of the Division to reach safety.

The afternoon dragged on. No Fascists came. My comrades seemed to start to think that the Battle of the Aragon was now over and that the Rebels wouldn't push on through into Catalunya after all. I felt differently. I thought that the Italians in Calaceite were just licking their wounds after the morning bombing. They were burying their dead, caring for their wounded, clearing rubble from the streets so that their tanks could get through. They would push on soon enough. And they would be angry. They would be mad that they had been bombed. They would be looking for revenge. And our little group would be the first to feel their wrath. We would be wiped out. No prisoners would be taken.

Eventually, the evening faded into darkness and we all breathed that sigh of relief that all soldiers do. We had survived through to the end of another difficult day. The others had a small amount of water which was shared around so that at least I had a small drink. There was no food. No one had any food. Or at least they kept quiet about it. It was reckoned that all soldiers had some item of food stashed away somewhere for emergency's sake, but I didn't believe that. I felt that if I had food, I was going to eat it, all of it. I didn't want to die with food still hidden away, what a waste. I certainly didn't want to leave anything for the Fascist vultures to find when they picked me over. Jack had died with a large piece of chorizo hidden in his ammunition pouch. I could have done the same. What I wouldn't have given at that moment for a piece of the old woman's chorizo. Tough as boots and tasting like it was rancid. It would have been a veritable feast.

Now that it was dark, my comrades seemed to relax a little. Cigarettes were shared and talk turned to home and to their loved ones, imagined or real. A lot of soldiers latched onto the memory of some girl they may have once spoken to or maybe only just seen the one time and turned her into their sweetheart. She probably didn't even know that they existed. She certainly wouldn't give a damn whether they got blown to pieces in Spain or not. Imagine when the poor lad got back to his dreary village, and he found that she was married with four kids. I think I was lucky that I had never known any girls that I wanted to fantasise about. I had enough on my mind without being tormented in my dreams by a girl, however beautiful I might imagine her to be. I hoped that I would never be interested in girls, they only brought trouble.

No watch was going to be set. No one believed that the Fascists would advance in the dark. Everyone agreed that they would wait until dawn and that it was better to sleep and be up early, ready and waiting for them. I said I would keep watch by the road just in case, I never slept much anyway I said. Which was true. One of the men handed me his rifle and his ammunition pouch, just in case. That was a good idea I thought.

"Try not to shoot any of ours," he said with a smile. I frowned at him. I didn't really want to be reminded of how my friend had been killed.

I distanced myself from the others, climbing over the boulders and out of sight. I found a safe spot and settled down to wait. The night was dark. Scudding clouds masked and then unmasked the pale moon.

After what I judged to be about an hour, I decided that I had waited long enough. I got cautiously to my feet and paused to listen. I could hear the rumble of snoring from behind the boulders and I took that to be a good sign. As quietly as I could, I slipped away into the night. I felt bad about taking someone else's weapon and leaving him to face the enemy the next day without it, but I figured I might need it. If he ever caught up with me again, he would more than likely rip my head off. Still, the more I had thought about it, the more I had convinced myself that they would just be slaughtered the next day.

I crept along the road, making as little noise as possible, until I thought I was out of earshot. Was I now a deserter? I didn't think so. I wasn't running away from the war, just trying to re-join the main body of our army and leave behind a bunch of my fellow countrymen who had, it seemed to me, gone quite mad. Who would thank them for throwing away their lives in such a useless situation? The Republic? The politicians in Valencia? The Spanish people? No. No one would give a damn. That was why I had decided not to hang around.

The road climbed up towards the Coll del Moro which was the highest ground around. It was earie walking along the road through the pine forest. I kept imaging the ghosts of the people who had once lived up there, flitting between the trees around me. Had they made their home in such an inhospitable place to keep them safe from the Romans? Or were they from a previous time even to that? I didn't know. It was just scary being alone. Maybe I shouldn't have gone off by myself after all. I even toyed with the idea of creeping back to the crossroads and hoping that the others hadn't missed me. In the end, I pressed on, taking what little courage I had in both hands and longing for daylight.

Dropping down from the high ground I saw Gandesa before me, its tall thin church tower reaching imploringly up into the night sky. It was obvious even from a distance, that the Battle for Gandesa was over. There were smouldering buildings and carts pulled by donkeys were laden with bodies. They were taking them out of the town before dawn so that the civilian population wouldn't be alarmed. I saw several men being marched towards the little cemetery at gunpoint.

The Rebels had obviously got to Gandesa first by the other route, from Batea to Corbera d'Ebre directly and not through the pass of the Coll del Moro. That meant that Batea had fallen and that made me sad. I think if I could have, I would have liked to have stayed there forever. Not only would I have been near to Jack, but I could have stayed at the convalescence home and been pampered by the nurses or just left to sleep my life away in the little internal patio with its dusty geraniums.

It also meant that Corbera d'Ebre had fallen too. It filled me with a sudden panic. Corbera had been my backup plan if I found Gandesa in hostile hands. Where could I go to now? I sat down to rest and to think. It had been a long night, walking on my own and my morale was low. I hadn't had anything to eat. I guess I felt sorry for myself. I sat down on a rock and watched the activity in Gandesa down below. What would Walt do now I wondered? What would Jack do? I could curl myself up into a ball and go to sleep on a bed of pine needles and wait to be found by the enemy and shot, or I could somehow find the strength to carry on.

I thought back over everything I had been through. The battle for the ruins of Belchite, the never-ending trek across the Aragon, to villages and towns whose names I had now forgotten, only to arrive at each and find them already gone. The death of Walt and the pointless loss of my best friend, my only friend. Had it all been for nothing? It couldn't have been. I could have died a thousand times, but somehow, I was still alive. That must mean something, mustn't it?

From Gandesa, I knew there was another road, a minor one that skirted between the Serra de Pandols and the Serra de Cavalls, I had seen it when we had marched past. I couldn't remember the name of the village on a signpost that pointed away from the Gandesa to Corbera road, but that route seemed my only hope of reaching safety. It had to lead to the river. If I could cross the Ebro, then I would be back in friendly territory, at least I hoped it would still be friendly.

The most dangerous part of my journey was going to be the first part. I decided to waste no more time. I had to skirt around Gandesa and pick up the road through the hills before it was completely light. Sure, I was cold, I was hungry, and I was miserable, but that was all beside the point. Come the dawn I would stick out like a sore thumb.

The road I wanted, split from the main road in the centre of Gandesa, so I turned south, walking across fields and clambering over low stone walls. Eventually, I saw the road and walked away from the outskirts of the town as quickly as possible. It was just starting to get light. It was possible that the whole of the Fascist army would choose to follow me towards the Ebro, I just had to hope that they took the main road instead.

The surface of the road was uneven and unloved, but it was better than walking across country. It twisted through the gap between the two ranges of hills and hopefully towards the Ebro. How far was it to the river? I didn't have a clue, I just hoped it wasn't too far.

After an hour or so of walking, I came to a little stream where I could at least have a drink and wash my face. I still had no water bottle, but fortunately the stream seemed to want to follow the road as far into the distance as I could see. It must be a tiny tributary of the Ebro and having it close by on my righthand side was reassuring. It meant that I was heading in the right direction and that I could get a drink of water from time to time.

By around midday, I was forced to make a choice. The road and the stream parted company. The road wanted to continue south, but the stream headed east. I decided that the stream would know the way to the river, whilst the road might lead somewhere else. Besides, I needed freshwater, and following the road seemed the more dangerous option.

So, I walked along by the stream for a while. There were no signs of human activity for some time, until eventually I came to a small cluster of farms close together. It wasn't really a village, just a group of people who had decided to establish their smallholdings close to the stream and close to one another. There were orchards of trees planted in neat rows, their branches green with the first buds of spring. I decided that I had to eat something, anything, and so I approached the first house. I left my gun a little way off, leaning against an olive tree so as not to startle the occupants.

I knocked on the wooden door of the house and waited. A woman with a baby in her arms opened after a while. I saw the shock on her face when she saw me. I held out my hands to show that I was unarmed. She started to say things at me, words tumbling from her mouth like a waterfall.

"Hambre," I said quietly.

She calmed down a bit and looked into my eyes. I wasn't dangerous she must have decided. She stepped back from the door and allowed me to enter her house. Inside it was dark, and my eyes took a moment to adjust. I saw an old man sitting in an armchair, his eyes staring, his mouth hanging open. Moaning to himself. He didn't register my arrival. The woman pointed for me to sit at a small table in the centre of the room. There was a fireplace and hanging above the fire was a cooking pot. Something smelt good.

The woman disappeared into another room and came back without her baby. Then she found a bowl and ladled out some of the soup that was in the cooking pot. She placed the bowl in front of me and handed me an old spoon. Then she sat down to watch me eat, her large brown eyes never leaving my face. She had probably never seen anyone like me before I thought. I wondered where her husband might be. Probably he had been a soldier, probably he was dead. Although, she might not know it yet.

The soup was hot, but I wasn't going to wait for it to cool down, my stomach wouldn't let me. It tasted of earth, but there were small pieces of carrot and some chunks of a green vegetable that I didn't know what it was, it tasted a bit like celery though. And of course, there were white beans. I ate it all in a matter of minutes. I could have eaten the whole pot, but I couldn't leave the woman and the old man with nothing. I stood to leave. The woman smiled and got up from the table to accompany me to the door.

"Gracias," I said.

"Vaya con Dios," she replied with a sad smile. Then she pointed to a little track that headed off in a north easterly direction. "Miravet," she told me slowly and then repeated the name to make sure I understood. I guessed it was the name of a village. She seemed to want me to go there, even though the stream went in a different direction. I nodded and thanked her again. I collected my rifle from where I had left it and set off along the track. It was one thing to follow the stream to the Ebro, it would be a totally different thing to be able to cross the river. I couldn't swim, so I needed to find a bridge. Maybe there was a bridge at Miravet, anyway, there was only one way to find out.

CHAPTER TWENTY-ONE

I felt a lot better after having had something to eat. It was amazing what a plate of simple food could do to lift the spirits. I hurried now in the early afternoon, whereas I had dragged my feet throughout the long morning. I had been dead tired after walking most of the night, but now I felt alive again.

There were small hills to the right of the track, lower than those I had walked through the previous day. It was hot now, and I was soon starting to regret having abandoned the stream. However, as luck would have it, after walking about five miles, another stream appeared and wanted to follow my path. I drank my fill of the cold water and washed my head. I had no hat to protect me from the sun, having left it behind in the cuartel back in Calaceite. All I had with me now were the clothes I wore and a stolen rifle and ammunition pouch.

The track wound between rocky cliffs and I trudged on through the afternoon. Then, suddenly, round a bend I saw a town. And there, wide and grey, cutting through the forests on either bank was the great River Ebro. I had heard so much about it but had never thought I would see it for real. It was more formidable than I had assumed it would be, like a great grey dragon lying out full length across the landscape. All-consuming.

The town of Miravet was dominated by a castle, up on top of a huge cliff of bright stone dotted with cactus plants. About halfway down the cliff was the church and then below and downwards to the river were the houses. They were tall and thin, three or even four storeys, clinging to the cliff. As I approached, I came to a roadblock which was no surprise. They saw that I was alone, and it was obvious that I was a foreigner.

One of the men approached to talk to me. I didn't understand him, I just said "Brigadista," and he patted me on the back and led me through the roadblock and pointed up at the castle. He made a gesture whilst trying to explain to me that I should go there.

I walked along the road and into the town. The streets were narrow and shaded by the tall houses. I didn't know which way to go, but I figured if I just kept climbing, I would eventually come to the castle. At the end of a street that was made up of wide stone steps I reached the little square beside the church. I looked over the edge of the balcony and saw the river below. Looking upwards, I could see the castle and a steep track climbing towards it.

I made my way along the track, ascending the rockface. Sometimes, there were steps cut into the rock, at other times it was just loose stones. I worried about slipping. There were bright green cactus plants and straggling bare bushes clinging on to the side of the cliff for dear life. It was a long climb and I was already exhausted. It seemed to take forever.

When at last I reached the top of the track, I found the huge walls of the castle reaching up above me, blocking out the sunshine. A young soldier approached me and, when he realised that I couldn't understand his greeting, he simply beckoned for me to follow him. We skirted around the walls until we came to a small entrance to the castle.

Inside, all was hustle and bustle, soldiers moving around looking busy. Wooden ammunition crates and boxes of different sizes were being loaded into the back of open lorries. Miravet castle had been used to store supplies and ammunition safe within its sturdy walls, but now it was obviously going to be abandoned. The Loyalist forces were preparing to retreat to the other side of the Ebro and use it as a natural line of defence to try to halt the rampaging Rebel war machine.

The soldier led me over to the man who was supervising the loading of the lorries. They talked briefly and I caught the word Brigadista. Then the soldier left us.

"Inglés?" the man asked me. I nodded.

"Internacionales," I told him. "Fifteeth Brigade."

"Yes, your friends are in Mora d'Ebre," he said slowly. He pointed to the first lorry. "Go." He gave me a smile and a nod.

I climbed up onto the back of the lorry and as soon as it was fully loaded, we left Miravet. From the main entrance to the castle, there was a road that wound down the back of the cliff and around behind the houses to come out down by the river. There it joined up with the road to Mora d'Ebre. We went through a final roadblock and then we were off towards Mora, alongside the river. The lorry lurched violently from side to side and I had to wedge myself between the crates of ammunition to stop from being thrown violently from side to side. In the end, out of sheer exhaustion, I curled myself up and managed to fall asleep, despite the uncomfortable position I had adopted.

*

I was awoken by the driver sometime later, to tell me that we had arrived. It was late afternoon. We were inside another castle, this time in Mora d'Ebre. My body felt battered and bruised from the awful journey and I stretched myself stiffly once I had climbed down from the back of the lorry. I would be sore for days I thought.

The driver led me across the wide courtyard to a small awning. Seated at a desk looking at some documents was a man I recognised.

"Well, well, well," he said with a smile of recognition. "Billy Bird if I'm not mistaken."

"Yes comrade," I replied.

"So, what 'appened to you this time son? Says 'ere on my list that you're missing presumed dead."

"I was taken prisoner in Calaceite, but I escaped and managed to get to Miravet. Then I came 'ere on that lorry." I pointed over across the courtyard at the lorry that was just leaving to take its supplies across the bridge into Mora la Nueva on the other side of the river.

"You came all this way on your own?" he asked. I could see he doubted my story.

"Yes comrade." I wanted to tell him about the massacre in Calaceite and about the others being put on lorries and taken away somewhere by the Guardia Civil. I wanted to tell him about the handful of Britishers that I had left behind at the crossroads of the road to Batea and how they planned to make a brave and desperate last stand. But in the end, I told him nothing. I didn't think he would have believed me anyway. I didn't want to make myself out to appear to be a deserter or a traitor or worse still a coward. I think that was what he thought I was, a coward. He probably assumed that as soon as there was the first sign of a battle I just ran away. But he had no proof of that, and quite miraculously I had made it back to our own lines by myself. Maybe I was a Fascist spy. Maybe I had somehow led the British Battalion into the ambush at Calaceite. I was relieved when he crossed out the word 'missing' that had been written next to my name on his list.

"We've lost a lot of good men, Billy," he said with a sigh. "Too many. I've got over three hundred still not accounted for."

"It's sad," I said.

"It's a tragedy."

"Yes, comrade."

"Well, you made it out alive. Somehow. And just in time too. We're pulling out first thing in the morning."

"Are we going to surrender?"

"No lad. We're going to blow the bridge tomorrow at noon and that should keep Franco at bay for a while."

I didn't think that blowing a bridge was going to keep the Rebels at bay for very long, certainly not the German and Italian planes that had harried us out of the Aragon, but again I said nothing.

"Where do I go?" I asked him.

"I'm finished 'ere for the day. I don't think anyone else will arrive now. I'll take you to join the others. I expect you could do with somethin' to eat."

"That'd be great," I said.

We left the castle with its rounded towers and headed alongside the river into the heart of the town. The streets were narrow, and we saw no one. The civilian population would have left already to cross over the river to safety. Only soldiers and maybe a few Fascist sympathisers remained, hidden away, awaiting the arrival of the Rebels and the establishment of the new regime.

What was left of the British Battalion was billeted in a small house not far from the bridge. Some men were standing in the doorway, smoking.

"'Ere, Billy lad, 'ave you seen…?" they asked me and reeled off a list of names of people I had no knowledge of. I just shook my head apologetically.

Inside, I was given a place to bed down on a blanket on the floor in an upstairs room. There were no mattresses. I lay down and waited for food to arrive. I was too tired to even take my boots off let alone have a wash.

*

The next morning, we were woken early. Once we had drunk some foul coffee and forced down a piece of stale bread, we took our things across the bridge to Mora la Nueva. Then we returned to help move anything else that needed taking. The bridge was a hive of activity. I just hoped that the German Stukas wouldn't choose that morning to come to bomb it.

We dodged between the last lorries or laden donkeys, an ambulance taking the wounded to safety. Just before twelve, the bridge was cleared. A last check was carried out in Mora d'Ebre that there was no one left behind, and then we all spread out along the riverbank at a safe distance to watch the bridge being blown. A British engineer and a team of Spanish dinamiteros had placed the explosives and were standing by to detonate their charges. I thought it was exciting. I'd never been a witness to something as spectacular as blowing up a bridge before.

The bridge crossed the river on a series of huge stone pillars, on top of which for most of its length was a sort of iron cage. It looked so strong.

At precisely noon, the charges were blown. There was a quick series of rolling explosions. The noise was deafening. I felt the blast slap me in the face. The iron cage seemed to rise into the air, split into pieces and then slump slowly down into the river. It was certainly smashed beyond repair that was for sure. The Rebels wouldn't be able to use it to cross the Ebro now.

It was 3rd April 1938. On the same day as they blew the bridge at Mora d'Ebre, the Nationalist army reached the Mediterranean at Viñaroz, so cutting Catalunya off from the rest of the Republican zone.

As I watched the huge dust cloud settle over the twisted iron remains of the bridge, I felt that the nightmare of the Aragon retreat was finally over. What would happen to Catalunya I did not know. Nor did I know that not many months later we would be back across the Ebro to fight once more to try to recapture the same towns we had just abandoned. The Battle of the Aragon was over, but the Battle of the Ebro was still to be fought.

By the same author…

Spanish Civil War Novels

THE LAST LORRY

TEARS IN THE EBRO

Other Novels

THE FORGOTTEN FOOTBALLER

THE TALLEST TOWER

Poetry

A SPITFIRE IN THE CLOUDS

A GIRL FROM THE MOUNTAINS

MY WEBSITE IS: kelvinhughesauthor.wix.com/author-blog

Follow me on FaceBook: kelvin hughes - writer

Printed in Great Britain
by Amazon